FIRST LOVE

"A date?" Nancy Fox exclaimed when her daughter told her the news that evening. "Who with?"

"A boy at work. He's—"

"A local boy?" her mother said, making it sound as if Tracy were going to date a gorilla.

"Yes," said Tracy excitedly. "I'm kind of glad he asked me today because I think it'd be good if we sort of forget about fixing me up with your friends' sons this summer."

"I don't know if I can do that, Tracy," her mother said. "I'm not even sure I like the idea of this boy at all."

"How can you say that? You don't even know him," Tracy shot back.

"Do *you*?" her mother asked. "You haven't been on the job very long—you can't know much about him."

"I've been working two whole weeks. And we talk to each other every day," Tracy said. "We're friends!" She felt close to tears. What if her mother wouldn't let her go?

Bantam Sweet Dreams Romances
Ask your bookseller for the books you have missed

First Love

Debra Spector

BANTAM BOOKS
TORONTO • NEW YORK • LONDON • SYDNEY

RL 7, IL age 11 and up

FIRST LOVE
A Bantam Book / June 1983

Cover photo by Pat Hill

ISBN 0-553-23509-5

Published simultaneously in the United States and Canada

*Bantam Books are published by Bantam Books, Inc. Its trademark,
consisting of the words "Bantam Books" and the portrayal of a
rooster, is Registered in U.S. Patent and Trademark Office and in
other countries. Marca Registrada. Bantam Books, Inc., 666 Fifth
Avenue, New York, New York 10103.*

Made and printed in Great Britain by Hunt Barnard Printing Ltd.

O   0 9 8 7 6 5 4 3 2 1

First Love

Chapter One

Tracy Fox approached the white frame building at the end of the boardwalk: Captain Tony's Restaurant, a beachfront landmark for fifty years. Looking down at her new white waitress uniform, she wondered for a moment if she had the nerve to go inside. She had never waited on tables—in fact, this would be her first paying job ever.

About ten feet from the entrance she paused and looked intently at the old, weathered building set off by the early morning light. It was rather charming, she thought, the type of quaint structure that looked as if it would have been more appropriate off the coast of Maine than here in this small seaside town in New Jersey. True, the royal blue shutters looked as if they could use another coat of paint, and the fishnet framing the front door was full of tears, but Tracy was sure the owner would take care of these things during the next few weeks before the tourists started their annual summer onslaught.

Thinking of the crowds, she checked her watch for the tenth time since she left her house. It was six-forty; she had twenty minutes to decide if she really wanted to spend the most glorious days of the year hauling dirty dishes and listening to people complain about overcooked meat and chipped china.

But she knew she'd go through with it. Even though the job had been her mother's idea, Tracy wanted to work this summer. The money, although not much, was a plus, of course, but with most of her friends away for the summer, she was also looking forward to making new ones and expanding her horizons.

An ocean breeze blew softly through Tracy's shoulder-length brown hair. Tracy and her hair hadn't gotten along too well since she had started to let it grow long. It had a nasty tendency of frizzing up on her at the worst possible moments. Tracy lived for the days when it framed her narrow, oval face just right, making her look the way she thought a normal sixteen-year-old girl ought to look. Now, she combed her fingers through

2

her hair, hoping that was all it needed to stay the way she'd fixed it.

"Going in?" a voice behind her asked.

She gasped. She hadn't heard anyone come up behind her. Turning around, she saw a tall, slim boy with hair the color of wet sand looking at her questioningly.

"I'm David Saylor," he said. "I work here."

"You do?"

"Yeah. Don't I look the type?" He smiled, showing two dimples.

"I didn't know there was a type," Tracy said uncertainly. "Are you a waiter?"

"No way. I'm strictly a kitchen guy. But you look like you're dressed for service. This your first job?"

"I was hoping it didn't show," Tracy said, squinting into the morning sun to face David, who was half a foot taller than she. "My mom said I should find work this summer. In a fit of insanity I decided waiting tables might be fun—and they hired me. I certainly hope Mr. Parron and I are ready for each other."

"Well, Mr. Parron can get a little crazy sometimes, but you should do all right. What did you say your name was?"

"Tracy. Tracy Fox."

"Any relation to Nancy Fox?"

"As a matter of fact, yes. She's my mother." Tracy grimaced.

"Did I say something wrong?" David asked.

"No," Tracy said resignedly. "I should be used to being Nancy Fox's daughter after all these years. It's just that everyplace I go people are always asking if I'm related to her."

"I have to admit I've never heard her radio show. But my mother's a big fan. She listens all the time."

"You're from around here?"

He nodded. "A born-and-bred Port Henry native."

"Oh, one of our rivals."

"You must live here in Oceanside then."

The neighboring Oceanside and Port Henry high schools had been friendly rivals for as far back as anyone could remember.

"Yeah. I was born in New York, but Mom brought me down here so I wouldn't have to grow up in the hard, cruel city." She held her hand to her forehead in mock seriousness.

David grinned, then glanced at the old clock on the Oceanside bathhouse. "I'd better fire up the grills before Parron grills *me*." Turning to Tracy he asked pleasantly, "Coming?"

She shook her head. "I still have ten minutes of freedom."

"Catch you later, then," he said, smiling.

Not bad, Tracy thought. The job hadn't even started, and she'd already met a guy—a nice one. That was another reason she was looking forward to working at the restaurant. In fact, it was the main one as far as Tracy was concerned. She had made an informal pledge to her best friend Kate before Kate had gone away for the summer, that this would be the summer she would find *him*—"The Boy." In her sixteen years she hadn't met any boy who had lasted beyond the first date, but it was her secret hope that the restaurant would provide her the opportunity to meet all the boys she'd ever want to know. Now that she had met one, she couldn't wait to see who else might walk through the door.

Thinking about all the boys she might be working with, and boys who'd certainly be stopping in for a bite to eat, Tracy whiled away the time until seven, pacing between the restaurant and a nearby souvenir shop. But she didn't see the stone wedged between two weathered planks, and the next thing she knew, her too-long legs gave way, and she went sprawling on the boardwalk.

"Oh, Fillmore!" she exclaimed.

"Who's Fillmore?"

Tracy looked up to see a white-uniformed girl bending over her.

"Oh, no one," said Tracy disgustedly. "Fillmore's my swear word. It's the only one my mother won't go catatonic over."

"Oh. Are you all right?"

"Yes." Tracy could feel herself blushing. She straightened her uniform as she rose. Then, looking down at herself, she gasped. "What a mess!"

"It's not so bad—just some dust and sand." The girl took off her black-rimmed sunglasses and put them in a pocket of the oversized man's suit jacket she was wearing over her uniform.

"What do you mean?" Tracy was beginning to panic. "This is my first day on the job. I can't walk in there looking like this."

The girl considered that. "Is there any place we can go to get you cleaned off?"

Tracy thought a moment. Then, picking up her cloth bag, she led the other girl down the boardwalk to the public rest rooms in the bathhouse. On the way over she said, "You don't have to come with me, if you don't want."

"I don't mind. Since we're going to be working together at Captain Tony's this summer, we might as well get to know each other." She extended her hand. "I'm Jennifer Bradley."

"I'm Tracy Fox. I don't remember seeing you at school. You from around here?"

Jennifer shook her head. "I'm from Plainfield," she said as they entered the cavernous, old tiled bathhouse. "I'm spending the summer here with my grandmother. What about you?"

"I live here with my mother. This is my first job. I'm hoping I can sort of broaden my horizons this summer. You know, meet people. . . ."

"Like guys?" asked Jennifer, smiling.

"Well . . . yeah."

"You ought to be able to do that."

"I'm counting on it. In fact, I already met one." Tracy told her about David.

"He sounds like a good start," Jennifer said. "As long as you don't think 'clumsy,' you'll do all right."

Tracy grinned. She wet the smudges on her uniform and looked around for a paper towel. "Wouldn't you know it? All they have are those blowers. Now what am I going to do?"

"Simple." Jennifer opened her purse. "The first rule of travel is: always carry a handkerchief. Here."

"Thanks," Tracy said, wiping at the stains.

Jennifer noticed her surroundings for the first time. "I really like it in here. This place is gorgeous."

Tracy looked at her oddly. "The *bathroom*?"

"No, I mean this tile. Look at that border, the detail in each individual piece. It's a work of art." Jennifer slid her fingers over the raised tiles.

"This old place? I heard somewhere they're thinking of tearing it down at the end of the summer."

"They can't!" Jennifer said with a vehemence that surprised Tracy. "Sure it may be a little run-down, and some of the fixtures need to be replaced, but they can't get rid of the whole building. Can't they see it's a cultural landmark?"

"Not this town." Tracy checked her watch again. "Yipes! Let's go! We're going to be late."

The two girls ran down the boardwalk. They pulled open the wood-plank door at seven o'clock sharp and joined four other waitresses lined up in the lobby. Standing before them was a short, rumpled man fingering a cigar. There were no boys in sight.

"Good morning, girls," the man said, without a hint of a smile. "I'd like to welcome you newcomers to Captain Tony's. I'm Walter Parron, the owner and manager, and this is Hilda Swanson, our supervisor of waitresses." He pointed to one of the waitresses, a tall, heavyset woman with upswept gray hair set like a helmet. She handed each of them a royal blue apron. In the pocket of each was an order pad and a pencil.

Mr. Parron continued his speech. "We don't have much time. The doors open at seven-thirty, and you'll remain on duty until the night shift comes on at three. Hilda will show you new girls the ropes and assign you your stations. You regulars know your responsibilities." He walked over to the cash register. Then, glancing at Tracy and Jennifer, he said, "I'll be watching you."

"He's going to be tough," Tracy whispered on their way over to the gray-haired lady.

"I've seen tougher," Jennifer said. "Don't worry too much."

At the other side of the wood-beamed restaurant, Hilda gave them their instructions. "Each of you will be responsible for four tables. I'm in charge of seating, and I try to spread out the customers so none of you will be unduly burdened. But I have to warn you that at times the place will be filled to capacity, and you're going to have to be on your toes. Understand?"

The girls nodded.

Hilda's expression softened. "I know it sounds rough, but once you master the routine it won't be so bad. Any questions?"

"Was there really a Captain Tony?" asked Sandy, a waitress who looked a little older than Jennifer.

"Oh, yes," said Hilda. "And a fine man he was. Generous with his food, generous with his customers, and, of course, with his help."

"What happened to him?" Jennifer asked.

"He died," Hilda said sadly. "And then *he* took over." She cast a disgusted look at Mr. Parron, who was counting change in the register. "I hope you girls like to work."

When the restaurant opened, Tracy planted herself by the wooden railing that separated the bar from the dining room, nervously awaiting her first customers, while Jennifer, Hilda, and Sandy were already busy with early morning arrivals. One of the other waitresses, Margaret, a brassy redhead who looked as if she would have been more at home in a cocktail lounge, was deep in conversation with Mr. Parron. The only other waitress, Gertrude, a short, stooped woman who smelled of onions, was polishing the barware as she examined the racing results in the local newspaper.

Finally Hilda led someone to one of Tracy's tables overlooking the ocean. "Good morning," Tracy said, taking her order pad out of the pocket of her apron. "What can I get you?"

"A menu would be nice," the gravel-voiced woman said.

"Oh, of course." Tracy ran off and returned with a laminated sheet. She waited while the woman scanned the menu. "The scrambled eggs are good," she said, not really sure if that was true.

"That won't be necessary," the woman said, still regarding the menu. She had more rings on her fingers than Tracy could count. "Just bring me some coffee and an apple danish." She handed the menu to Tracy.

"Oh, thank you!" Tracy said, relieved.

The woman eyed her curiously. "I'm the one who's supposed to do the thanking around here."

"I'm sorry," Tracy explained. "You see, you're my first customer, and I'm just glad your order is so easy to fill."

The woman smiled. "I'll take my coffee black, too."

"Yes, ma'am."

"Call me Mrs. Logan," the woman said, still smiling.

Later, Tracy was pleased to see the fifty cents Mrs. Logan left her. Pocketing the change, she thought: I hope all my customers are generous.

"Hey, this is going to be fun," she whispered to Jennifer on the way to the kitchen after the breakfast rush was over. So far she'd served five customers without any trouble.

Jennifer blew a stray lock of hair off her forehead and shook her head. "This must be your lucky day. I just got done serving a whiny woman and her three bratty kids. I call that work."

Tracy, who was looking at Jennifer, didn't see Margaret coming out of the kitchen as she was going in. "Hey, watch it, will you?" Margaret cried.

"Sorry," Tracy said contritely but rolled her eyes at Jennifer. She whispered, "Margaret acts like she *owns* this place."

"That's not surprising. Hilda says she's been here forever. In fact, she's already told me Margaret's got a thing going with Mr. Parron."

"You're kidding! Where's her taste?"

"Where's his?" The girls giggled.

As soon as the breakfast crowd thinned out, it was time to set up for lunch. Hilda showed the girls where to find the lunch menus and the postings for the specials of the day, leaving Tracy no time to concentrate on anything but work.

Despite Jennifer's pronouncement and her own better judgment, Tracy was enjoying her job so far. She liked it when the truck

12

driver smiled back at her, when the elderly couple called her a "lovely girl," and when the middle-aged woman told her to "have a nice day." The best part was that none of them said a word about any little mistakes she made.

But the morning crowd did nothing to prepare Tracy for the onslaught at lunch. To fill in the lulls before the season got into full swing, Mr. Parron had arranged for busloads of tourists to descend upon Oceanside—one of their stops being Captain Tony's, naturally. Today's contingent, Tracy was told, was a church auxiliary.

Before Tracy had a chance to catch her breath, all her stations were full, leaving her with the dilemma of whom to serve first. Finally, because her tables were all next to each other, she decided just to start taking requests, then to serve the customers in the order of the requests. It worked fine for the first table, whose hamburger platters were easy to remember, but she started to feel flustered at the second table, with its four different orders and special requests for nongreasy french fries. Maybe, she thought, it would be better to work only two tables at a time.

Tracy ran to the kitchen and posted the orders on little clips along the aluminum barrier separating the waitresses from the cooks. She scribbled 2H on one slip and the orders from the second table on another sheet, then hurried back to take the orders from the remaining two tables.

When Tracy returned to the kitchen, she was surprised to see that table two's orders were done ahead of one's, but unquestioningly she piled them on a big tin tray to carry to the hungry customers. "This isn't going to be so bad," she told herself, as she gingerly maneuvered the tray out of the kitchen . . . just as Margaret was entering.

"Oh!" she cried as two dishes slipped off the tray and went crashing to the floor. Tears blurred her eyes as she looked down at the mess while trying to balance the tray.

Maybe waitressing wasn't going to be so easy after all.

Chapter Two

"Are you all right?"

Tracy glanced up to see David, his blue-gray eyes full of concern. He had rushed to her side as soon as he'd heard the crash.

"I'm fine," Tracy whispered. "You really don't have to help. I can handle it."

"Please, let me," he whispered, moving closer. "We'll get these things cleaned up before Parron sees them."

No sooner were the words out of his mouth than the potbellied man pushed through the kitchen door, Margaret standing smugly behind him.

"What's going on here?" he demanded.

"I—I had an accident, sir," Tracy said, looking at the floor. "I'm really sorry. I'll clean it up now."

"I knew it was a mistake hiring a sixteen-year-old," Mr. Parron said grimly. "I won't tolerate such carelessness, Miss Fox. I run a tight ship here, and waste is not allowed. I can't afford it."

"Yes, Mr. Parron. You're not going to fire me, are you?"

"I don't have many choices, do I?" He flicked the ashes of his cigar over the shattered dishes.

"Excuse me, Mr. Parron," David spoke up. "I've been watching Tracy all morning, and I think she's done all right for her first day. This was just an accident. It could have happened to anyone. It wouldn't be fair to fire her over an accident, would it?"

Mr. Parron looked uncertain, and his voice was considerably softer when he said, "All right, I'll let it go, but just this once. No more trouble like this from now on. Understand?"

"Yes. Oh, thank you, Mr. Parron! You'll see what a good job I can do. You won't regret it, really." She scooped up a few shards of china that lay near his feet.

Mr. Parron strode out of the kitchen without saying another word. Margaret glared at Tracy for a moment, before following him out the door. Tracy continued picking up the broken pieces, while David went to get a mop from the back room.

When he returned, Tracy smiled up at him. "Thanks. I don't know how you got him to back down, but I really appreciate it."

"It was nothing, really. This is my second summer here, and the old man likes my cooking. He's not going to do anything to make me mad."

"Why should that matter?" she asked, rising.

"I'll let you in on a secret." He lowered his voice. "Charlie over there is a bit of a drunk." He pointed to the cook, hunched over a steaming pot of chowder. "I keep an eye on him so he doesn't burn anything or do something crazy. Parron appreciates it, though he'll never admit it."

"Well, anyway, thank you for sticking up for me," Tracy said. She had cleaned up the broken dishes and was now wiping off her uniform with a damp cloth. "You know, he might have fired you, too."

"It was something I had to do," David declared. "Last summer I saw too many waitresses bullied into leaving this place every time Parron got into one of his moods. I didn't say anything then, but I promised myself I'd speak up this summer if he gave anyone a hard time."

"I'm sorry I made you live up to your promise so soon."

"Hey, don't worry about it. Now if I were you, I'd get back to those customers of yours before they start complaining."

"OK." Tracy put her towel down on a nearby rack and turned to the door.

"And one more thing. Over here." Tracy followed David back to the food bins. "This your ticket?" He showed her the order slip she'd marked "2H." Tracy nodded. "Just to make sure," he continued, "what's an 'H'?"

"Hamburger, of course."

"Hmm, I thought it might be, but next time try to be a little more specific, OK? It could just as easily have meant ham sandwiches or hot dogs." He handed her two steaming burger platters, still warm from the heat lamps.

Tracy blushed. "Sorry. I was in a rush."

"It's all right. I won't tell Parron. This is our secret." David smiled.

"You're a lifesaver, David," Tracy said, brightening. "How can I thank you?"

David was silent for a moment. "I'll think of something," he said, before shooing her out to her customers.

Tracy managed to survive the rest of the busy

afternoon. Jennifer helped her get through the mad lunch hour, cleaning off a few of Tracy's tables when she wasn't looking.

"I saw what Parron put you through," Jennifer said when Tracy discovered what she was doing. "It was the least I could do to help."

"I'll do the same for you," Tracy said.

"Let's hope you won't have to."

Tracy was grateful for the support and began to think she might actually make some new friends this summer. She promised herself she'd try to pay them back by becoming the best waitress she possibly could. By the end of the summer, she vowed, she'd be a pro!

Chapter Three

"**Y**ou should have heard my show today, Dina," Nancy Fox said enthusiastically as she dished a serving of hot chicken casserole onto her friend's dinner plate.

"What happened?" Dina knew she really didn't have to ask. Nancy loved to tell stories and didn't need prompting.

Nancy served Tracy and then herself as she continued. "A few days ago I got a call from the spokesperson for the Save New Jersey Society. From what he told me, they sounded like some kind of environmental group. You know how important that is to me, so I booked him for today's show. I told him to come down to the studio by noon. At twelve-fifty-five this man comes into Master Control wearing a gas mask and shouting the world is doomed."

20

"So you turned him around and showed him the exit?"

"That was my first thought," Nancy said, leaning back in her chair. "But it was five minutes to air time, and he was my only guest, so I figured why not take a chance? Besides," she added slyly, "I was dying to find out what his get-up was all about."

"And?" Dina asked.

"When we're on the air, he declares we're this far away from poisoning ourselves." Nancy held two fingers a quarter of an inch apart. "He insists our only hope is to evacuate New Jersey and set up new colonies in the South Pacific."

"A novel idea," Dina said dryly.

"Actually, a lot of what he had to say made sense," Nancy said. "But with that gas mask on, it was hard to take him seriously."

"You mean he left it on?"

"He claims he and his group always wear them. I'd love to see them all together sometime." Nancy rolled her eyes. "But he was effective. About a dozen people phoned in wanting to know where they could sign up."

"You're kidding!"

"It never fails. I always get my biggest response whenever I have a gloom-and-doom person on."

21

Tracy listened to her mother's story in silence, focusing her attention on her plate in front of her. She had heard it all before—today was certainly not the first time her mother had entertained a strange person on her daily talk show. Much as her mother would hate to admit it, she got a kick out of those guests and their way-out ideas almost as much as her audience did. ·

"By the way," Nancy added, "our engineer showed me the final plans for my remotes. Gopher said all we need is the go-ahead from the station manager, and we'll be broadcasting from the beach during July and August."

"How are you going to do that?" Dina asked.

"We'll set up a little studio outside the Seaside Avenue beach entrance. All I'll need is a microphone or two. Gopher will handle the rest. He's a genius with electronics. Me, all I know is that I speak into the mike and my voice goes out over the air. How it gets there will forever remain a mystery to me."

"Maybe you ought to have Gopher on as a guest someday," Dina suggested. "To explain it all to you."

"Too boring." Nancy laughed. "I'm really looking forward to the change of scenery, though. It'll give us a chance to mingle with

22

the tourists and talk with some of Oceanside's more colorful beach people."

"And you'll be able to get a tan, Mom,"
Tracy spoke up. "You're always saying how
much you hate being cooped up in that studio during the summer."

"That's right. It'll be a nice change." Nancy
glanced at her daughter. "You've been unusu-
ally quiet tonight."

"My mouth is tired," Tracy muttered. She
didn't particularly feel like talking, especially
about work, which she knew her mother and
Dina would want to hear about. "I've been
talking all day."

But Dina spoke up then. "Tracy, you started
work today, didn't you?"

"Yup."

"My goodness!" Nancy cried. "My little girl
enters the world of business, and here I am
monopolizing the conversation. How'd it go?"

"I guess it has to come out sooner or later.
I had a rotten day."

"What happened?" Nancy prodded gently.

"I dropped a tray of food."

"Oh, sweetie." Nancy clucked. "But what's
a broken plate or two? They're easily replaced."
She reached over and took Tracy's hand.

Tracy looked up, surprised. "You're not mad
at me?"

23

Nancy put her hands on her hips. "Now why should I be mad at you? You had an accident, right?"

"Yeah."

"You're only human. Those things happen to the best of us. You'll do better tomorrow." Nancy paused. "I've about run out of motherly platitudes."

"You forgot better luck next time," Tracy suggested.

"See, you know all these things already. What do you need a mother for?" Nancy rose, straightening her black caftan. "Dina, care for some coffee?"

"I'd love some," her friend said.

When Nancy returned a few moments later with two steaming mugs, she gave her attention to Tracy again. "Tell me. Did anything *good* happen at work today?"

"One customer gave me a good tip. And there are some neat people there. There's this one waitress, Jennifer. She's eighteen, and she's spending the summer here with her grandmother, and she's into antiques and stuff like that. Also, I met this boy—"

Nancy smacked her head. "Tracy, I don't know where my brain has been today. You've just reminded me. . . . Oh, how could I have forgotten to tell you?"

"What, Mom?" Tracy realized she'd have to talk about David later. When her mother had an announcement to make, everything else in life had to be put on hold.

"Do you remember Garrett Boniface?" Nancy looked as if she were ready to burst.

"No," Tracy answered.

"He was a dear friend of your father's. They grew up together, in fact. He's done quite well for himself over the years, made a fortune in real estate, investments, that sort of thing."

Tracy didn't say anything. Her father had died when she was six months old, the victim of an accident at a Manhattan construction site. He wasn't much more than a name to her, and she couldn't care less about this stuffy old Garrett Whats-his-face.

"Now, Tracy," Nancy said when Tracy continued to remain silent, "Garrett has been very thoughtful to me over the years. Anyway, he's going to be racing in the Fourth of July regatta at Bright Cove next weekend, and he's bringing his family down from Connecticut with him."

"Are they staying with us?" Tracy wondered how they'd fit an entire family in their tiny house.

"No. But Garrett asked me if you wouldn't

mind spending that Saturday evening with his seventeen-year-old son."

"You didn't say yes, did you?" Tracy groaned.

"Of course I did. Avery is a handsome boy. Polite, well mannered, intelligent—I couldn't think of one reason why you wouldn't want to go out with him."

Tracy stared at her mother. "But . . . I don't even know him."

Nancy looked at Tracy thoughtfully. "I think Avery Boniface is exactly what the doctor ordered, young lady. You could use some confidence where boys are concerned. Avery is perfect. I'm sure you two will get along fine. You'll have lots to talk about—"

"Like what?" Tracy interrupted.

"His father was your father's friend . . ."

"I didn't know my father, either."

"So you can ask Avery, see?"

"Mom, it won't work. No boy works out. What makes you think Avery's going to be different?"

"Because a boy with his background knows the proper way to treat a young lady. You've just had too much experience with the wrong kind of boy." She sighed. "Sometimes I wish I'd never moved you to this hick town."

"It's not a hick town. I like it here," Tracy insisted.

Nancy got up, ran a hand through her soft hair, and paced the dining room as Tracy and Dina watched. "No, I think it was wrong to move you out of New York. The boys down here are too unsophisticated. They don't appreciate you. You should be exposed to boys with style and charm, boys who'd love to know a girl like you. But"—Tracy paid close attention to her mother's next words—"maybe it's not too late. Let me see what I can do. I've got some friends with teenage sons who'd love to meet an attractive girl. Of course, the beach is a good drawing card, too." From her expression Tracy could tell Nancy was falling in love with the idea as she went along.

"Mo-om—"

"Don't 'Mom' me, Tracy. By the end of summer you'll have no problem attracting any boy you want. Sometimes mothers can be right, you know."

"But, Nancy, if Tracy doesn't want—" Dina began.

She was quickly cut off. "Dina, don't you remember when you were sixteen, and you thought you knew all there was to know about life? Well, I do, and if I had a dollar for every wrong decision I made at that age, I could have retired years ago." Nancy folded her arms

27

across her chest—which meant the subject was closed.

Tracy didn't see any way out. It was hard enough to say no to her mother under normal circumstances, but when Nancy made up her mind about something, it would be as foolish to defy her as it would be to run in front of a speeding train. Besides, deep down Tracy couldn't think of a good reason not to go out on this date. This was, after all, the summer she was going to find *him*, and he might even turn out to be Avery, if she put her mind to it. As Tracy cleared the table, she decided there was no reason to fight it.

"So what do you say, Tracy?" asked her mother later.

"Which of my outfits do you think Avery will like?"

Nancy beamed her approval.

Chapter Four

The following morning Tracy greeted her first customer with a weary smile. "Menu, sir?" she asked.

The elderly gentleman straightened his red bow tie and smiled. "I've been coming here since nineteen forty-five, young lady. Know it back and forth. Let me have two scrambled eggs and a side of bacon."

Tracy rushed in the order, taking care to write legibly so there would be no confusion about what the man wanted. As she slipped the order into its clip, she was surprised to see David turn around and give her a big smile. "Morning, Tracy," he said.

"Hi, David. I've got another bacon and egg order for you." She eyed the mound of scrambled eggs cooking on one side of the grill, strips of bacon sizzling on the other.

"Somehow that doesn't surprise me," he said dryly. "How are you making out today?"

"Fine, but this is only my first customer."

"Well, that's a start," he said. He leaned down so that his eyes were even with hers. "I'd like to see you for a couple of minutes as soon as things slow down, OK?"

"Tracy!" Margaret was so close, Tracy could feel her breathing down her neck. "This is a business, not a social club. Get out there. Now!"

"All right," Tracy said meekly. Turning back to David she whispered, "OK," before scurrying out of the kitchen.

She waited on several other customers, then picked up Mr. Olson's order. "These look good," he said as Tracy placed the plate in front of him.

"Would you like anything else?"

"Just the check. And a cab, of course, when I'm through."

"A cab?" she asked in surprise.

"Yes. And be sure to ask for number five. He's my favorite."

Shaking her head, Tracy went back to Hilda with the request. "Oh, yes," Hilda said. "We always call a taxi for him. The number's on the inside of the bar."

"But why?" Tracy asked.

Hilda sighed. "Mr. Olson was a close friend of old Captain Tony. Parron feels a bit of an obligation to the poor fellow."

"You mean Parron's got a heart?"

"He let you keep your job, didn't he?" Hilda patted Tracy on the back. "Now run along before he changes his mind."

Several hours later, when the restaurant had cleared of most of its early customers, Tracy rushed to the kitchen, while the other waitresses retired to the back of the restaurant to relax or freshen up for the lunch crowd. Standing on tiptoe, she peered through the divider separating the cooks from the serving area and whispered, "David."

"Tracy." David looked up from the grill, where he was scraping away the remnants of breakfast food, and smiled. "Be with you in a minute."

Tracy stood back and read the restaurant code posted on the wall near the door while she waited for David to come out. She nearly gasped when, at last, he stood beside her. In all of the commotion the day before, she hadn't really noticed how tall and graceful he looked or how his light brown hair gently rested over the tops of his ears the way she thought all boys' hair should. "Glad you could make it," he said.

"Me, too. It sure was a busy morning."

Once, after a particularly awkward date, Tracy sat at her desk and wrote down all the clever opening lines she always wanted to use with boys. She vowed to memorize them so that she'd never be stuck for something to say to a boy she hardly knew. Now she couldn't think of one of them.

"It sure was," David said, sounding almost as awkward. For a second Tracy thought maybe he was as uncomfortable with girls as she was with boys, but she quickly dismissed that. No boy this good-looking could ever be at a loss with girls.

"I just thought," he continued, reaching for a large metal serving tray, "that before the lunchtime rush, you might like a pointer or two on how to handle one of these things. I know Parron thinks every girl who walks in here is a born waitress, but not everyone's perfect the first time."

"Did Parron put you up to this?" Tracy asked, a mixture of anger and hurt boiling up inside her. She didn't like the idea of playing student to his teacher. It made her feel stupid.

"Of course not," David replied. "I just think you're inexperienced—which everyone is when they first start out. Can you honestly tell me you know how to carry a full tray the right way? Did anyone ever show you?"

Tracy didn't have a comeback; she knew David had a valid point. "No," she said quietly. "OK, what do I do?"

David took the tray and a few empty plates and showed Tracy the proper way to stack them so the load would be balanced. Then he showed her the easiest way to lift it to her shoulder, carry it, and then serve her customers.

"Now, you try it," he said, handing her the tray.

Tracy followed his instructions. It didn't seem so difficult once he'd shown her his method. Carrying the loaded tray around the kitchen, Tracy could feel her confidence growing. This was exactly the type of advice she needed if she was really serious about keeping her pledge to be a good waitress.

"You were right, David," she said. "This is a lot easier than the way I was doing it."

"See what a pointer or two can do?"

She put down the tray. "I hope you don't mind my asking, but why are you doing this?"

"I guess because no one else is. People like Parron and Hilda expect everyone to be pros from the start, as if waitressing is something a person was naturally born to do. I think you're going to be all right now." He gave her a reassuring smile.

"Was cooking the same for you?" Tracy asked, picking up the tray again.

"Sure," he said, showing off his dimples again. "These gas burners are really different from the electric stove at home. It took me awhile to learn how to fry up eggs and bacon that didn't come out black on both sides. But Charlie was real helpful to me, so I guess I wanted to see you get a fair break, too."

Just then the door opened, and Jennifer called, "Tracy, are you in here?"

"Yeah," she answered, making a face at David. What now?

"You've got customers. Better come out before anyone notices."

In a flash Tracy handed the tray back to David. "Thanks," she said. "This has been a big help. I'm sorry I snapped at you." She ran out before she could hear David's response.

Smiling broadly, Tracy approached her customers with enthusiasm. The change she felt was enormous. All she had needed was David's attention to her problem. She hoped David wouldn't take it the wrong way when she scribbled, *You're terrific!* on her third lunch order. The summer was shaping up after all.

Chapter Five

On Thursday, Tracy and Jennifer took off for the beach at Chalihook, a town several miles up the coast. Tracy had succeeded in convincing Jennifer that their boy-hunting prospects would be better there than in Oceanside, where the beach was populated mostly by vacationing families and the town's large senior citizen community.

Tracy had spent a good part of the previous summer at the Fifth Street beach with her friends Kate, April, and Joanie. But now, not wanting to surround Jennifer with fifteen-year-olds, she steered her toward the Seventh Street beach, where the older kids hung out. When she spotted the line of bare-chested boys at the beachfront hot dog stands, she knew she'd made the right decision.

"It was nice of Parron to let both of us have the day off today," Jennifer said as they spread their beach towels on the sand. The sun was shining brightly overhead, and all around them small groups of people lay glistening on towels, soaking up the rays.

"It sure was. It's a perfect day for the beach," Tracy said. "I suppose Parron can afford to do this until business picks up." Tracy plopped down on her towel and took off her T-shirt, revealing the navy blue-and-white striped one-piece she'd bought the night before. It had a little string tie at the waist, but Tracy didn't think it would disguise the fact that there was hardly any difference between her waist and her hips.

Jennifer, too, stripped down to her suit, a tiny black bikini. She was splashing tanning oil on her legs when Tracy turned around. "Pretty sexy," Tracy said, not without a trace of envy.

"Thanks," Jennifer said. "It's one of the advantages of being petite."

"You're going to have every guy on the beach looking at you. Can I borrow some of your oil?"

Jennifer poured a little into Tracy's hand. "I don't know about that, but at least I've got a fighting chance here."

"Yeah. Captain Tony's hasn't exactly been crawling with boys."

"That's putting it mildly."

Flicking on her transistor radio, Tracy leaned back and let the summer sun wash over her. She savored this moment, her first time out for the season, when the sensation of the sun's heat was still new and soothing. She felt as if she could lie on the beach forever. That feeling usually disappeared by mid-July, when the humidity rose, but for the time being it was wonderful.

After an hour, however, she was ready for a break. "I'm going in the water," she told Jennifer. "Coming?"

"I don't think so," Jennifer answered, raising herself up on her elbows. "This suit's not made for getting wet."

Shrugging, Tracy tiptoed around a crazy-quilt pattern of blankets and bodies until she reached the surf. The water was cold at first, but she ran in, diving under a wave and skimming along through the invigorating green water.

Tracy had no idea how long she stayed in the surf, riding the waves, but as she walked back up the beach, she noticed a boy walking away from her blanket.

"What did I miss?" she asked curiously, reaching for a towel.

"Tracy, the neatest thing just happened. I got a date for Saturday night!" Jennifer squealed, unable to hide her enthusiasm.

"That guy?" Tracy asked, pointing to the retreating figure.

"Yes! Can you believe it? We started talking after you left. You should have seen him, Tracy. He's really something."

"Congratulations," Tracy said. "Too bad he doesn't have a friend."

"Oh, you've got plenty of time to find a guy. Besides, isn't your mother fixing you up with someone?"

"Yeah, but did you ever hear of a mother coming up with someone you'd want to see more than once?"

"Well, you never know. And then again, there's always David."

"David?" Tracy looked at Jennifer questioningly.

"Don't pretend you don't know what I'm talking about. I think he likes you. And take it from me, he's worth having. I'd be pretty interested myself if he were a little older."

"All he did was give me a few waitressing tips and help me out of a jam with Parron. He was just being friendly."

"Tracy, come on. I've seen the way he looks at you. I have a feeling he's interested in more than friendship."

"Maybe," Tracy said, sounding more ambivalent than she felt. Lying back on her towel, she realized she'd been thinking about David quite a bit. And after his lesson the other day she'd begun to wonder what he was like away from the restaurant and whether he had a girlfriend. Now Jennifer made her wonder even more. "He likes you," Jennifer had told her. Tracy smiled at the thought. She certainly hoped Jennifer was right.

Chapter Six

Nancy Fox was beaming when she woke Tracy for work the following Sunday morning. "Come on, honey, it's a beautiful day."

Yawning, Tracy nodded absently, swung her legs over the side of the bed, and peered out her window. Already the sun was inching off the ocean on its climb to the top of the sky. "Looks like it's going to be a hot one," she said sleepily.

"They're predicting mid to high eighties."

"Ugh." Tracy stood up and reached for her robe. A hot day meant lots of beachgoers and boardwalk strollers.

And a busy day at Captain Tony's.

From the moment her shift started, Tracy worked at a breakneck pace to keep up with the orders. On Sundays the restaurant offered an "all you can eat" breakfast, which Tracy wanted to rename "all you can serve" as she dashed back and forth into the kitchen for second and even third helpings.

At one point she bounded into the kitchen to retrieve an order for Mrs. Logan, who was fast becoming one of her regulars. As she was putting the plates on her tray, she cast a quick glance at David, who was frying up eggs like a machine. She turned away quickly, hoping he hadn't caught her looking at him.

The past two mornings, Tracy had gone to great pains to avoid him. It wasn't that she didn't want to talk to him; in fact, the opposite was true. After her conversation with Jennifer at the beach, she had decided she would really like to get to know David better. She liked his way of making her smile and wondered just what was behind the twinkle in his eyes. But realizing that and acting on it were two different things. She was afraid if she got too close to him too quickly she'd scare him off.

But David must have spotted her out of the corner of his eye, for he put down his spatula and came over to the counter. "Hello, stranger." He smiled pleasantly, resting his arms on the aluminum divider.

"Hello," Tracy said, returning the smile.

"I haven't seen you around much lately," he said. "You're not mad at me for showing you how to carry the trays, are you?"

"Oh, no." She shook her head emphatically, at the same time trying to appear casual. "It's just been so busy recently, that's all."

"Don't be in too much of a hurry," he said. "Some people like to linger a little over their meals." He caught himself. "Not that I'm trying to tell you how to do your job or anything."

"No, that's all right," she answered. "I can use all the help I can get on days like today."

"In that case, here's another bit of wisdom. You'll get better tips if you keep smiling."

"I'll be sure to remember that." Then, looking over David's shoulder, she said, "I've got some advice for you, too. You better get back to your eggs before they turn to rubber."

"Right." David grinned, turning back to the grill. "Come visit when you're not too busy. We cooks get lonely back here."

Maybe I'll just do that, she thought as she left the kitchen.

Remembering his other bit of advice, she smiled as she approached the table. "Here are your eggs," she said brightly to Mrs. Logan, placing them in front of her.

43

"Why thank you, young lady."

"Enjoy your breakfast," Tracy added. "And the beautiful view."

Looking a little stunned, the woman turned and looked out at the ocean. Two sea gulls hovered over the white-capped waves, and a sightseeing boat rounded the rocky point where the Oceanside lighthouse stood. The woman smiled wistfully.

"I've got to run now," Tracy said, "but I'll be back in a few minutes to see if you need anything else." She headed happily for the egg-eating couple, pleased that she had brought a little bit of pleasure to Mrs. Logan.

The couple sent her back to the kitchen for more bacon. Tracy wanted to tell David how well his advice was working, but Margaret was standing right next to her, and she didn't dare. Instead, she ripped off a piece of paper from her order pad and scribbled on it, *It works, David*, and hoped he'd understand.

"Is there anything else I can get you?" she asked Mrs. Logan a few minutes later.

"Young lady, you've opened my eyes to beauty. That's the biggest gift anyone can give another person."

"It was nothing," Tracy said, her cheeks growing as red as her sunburned nose.

"But now you can get me a cup of tea."

Later, when Tracy cleaned off the table, she found two crisp dollar bills under the teacup.

"I think I've found the secret of making it in this place," she said to Jennifer when they found a free moment. "I got two big tips this morning, and all I did was smile and say a few friendly words."

"Lucky you," Jennifer said. "All I got were five tables full of bratty kids and a trucker who wanted to pick me up."

"I bet things will turn around this afternoon," Tracy said. "By the way, how'd your date go?"

"The worst. I would have been better off spending the night with a book."

"Maybe you'll meet someone nicer at the beach this week."

"Maybe, but I have a feeling it's not the best place to pick up guys." She leaned closer and whispered, "I saw you talking to David a little while ago."

"Yeah," Tracy said, barely hiding a smile. "I think he's interested in me. But I'm not sure how to let him know I'm interested in him. I don't want to look pushy."

"Don't worry about it. You know, you could always take matters into your own hands and ask *him* out."

Tracy's brown eyes widened. "Are you kidding? I'm having a hard enough time as it is."

"In that case, just be yourself, and he'll get the idea."

When Tracy went back into the kitchen to place an order, she found a note with TRACY written on top in big, red, Magic Marker letters. Quickly she opened it and read David's words: *I'm glad things are working out for you.*

Tracy tried to get David's attention, but he was bent busily over a stack of pancakes. *You work too hard,* she wrote on another note. *Doesn't Parron let you take any breaks?*

It took another four hours for things to calm down enough so David could answer Tracy's note. On one of her breaks he motioned her to the stool next to the grill, while he leaned on the tile wall opposite it.

"It's been some morning," he said, wiping his brow. "Well, this is it."

"This is what?" she asked.

"The break you say Parron doesn't give me. It's very short on a day like this."

"Is it always this busy on Sundays?"

"Ha! Wait until the Fourth. That'll make today look like goofing off."

"I better have things completely under control by then. I really am getting the hang of this job, though. Thanks to you, I should add."

"All you needed were the basics. You're more than capable of taking it from there."

Tracy had to leave the kitchen after that, but she had the feeling she'd be spending more free time with David in the days ahead.

Sure enough, over the next few days Tracy began to find plenty of extra reasons to run into the kitchen. During the mid-morning lull, when Margaret was chatting in the back of the dining room with Mr. Parron and Jennifer was taking a breather, Tracy would saunter into the kitchen and watch David prepare for the lunch meals. From their chats she learned that he was seventeen, going into his senior year at Port Henry High, and that he had a younger brother and sister—and no girlfriend at the moment. He was surprisingly easy to talk to—for a boy.

That Friday he handed her a brown paper bag. "Do you like cookies?" he asked.

She looked inside. "Love them." She took out an oval one topped with nuts and raisins and bit into it. "Mmm." She sighed. "Divine. Did you make these?"

"From scratch," he said. "I whipped them up last night. I thought you'd like to see I could do more than grill hamburgers."

"You ought to get Parron to let you make stuff like this for the restaurant." She took another bite. "On second thought, I take that back. These are too good for Captain Tony's. Can I have the recipe?"

"Maybe I'll give you a cooking lesson and show you my special baking secrets," he said.

"I'd like that."

"How does tomorrow night sound?"

Tracy was all ready to say yes when she remembered her date with Avery Boniface. Why was her timing so rotten? Her face fell, and she hoped David hadn't noticed. "I'd really like to, but I'm busy tomorrow night."

"Another guy?" David tried to smile.

Tracy didn't know what to say. "Oh, no," she lied quickly. "Nothing like that."

"Well," he said, sounding wounded.

"We'll do it some other time, OK?" Tracy asked hopefully.

"Sure," David said. "There'll be other times." He walked back to the grill, looking as disappointed as Tracy felt.

"Thanks for the cookies," she called. Returning to the dining room, Tracy sighed.

She hoped she hadn't blown it. She really liked David, but she had an awful feeling she might have discouraged him from pursuing her further. And all because of some guy named Avery Boniface whom she hadn't even met.

Chapter Seven

"Mom, do I *have* to wear this?" Tracy was standing in front of the full-length mirror in the bathroom.

"You look beautiful, dear," her mother said, fixing the wide, lacy collar on Tracy's white dress. "My gold chain would add just the right touch. Now where did I put it?" She began to rummage through the bobbie pins and nail files in the vanity drawer. "Hmm, I can never find anything when I need it. . . . Oh, here it is."

Tracy took the chain, grimacing at her reflection. She never felt comfortable in dresses, and she felt more awkward than ever in this ruffly outfit. It made her thin legs look as if they belonged to a flamingo. "Why can't I wear my new sundress? I look really good in that."

"There's nothing wrong with what you've got on. When I saw it in Pierson's window yesterday, I knew it would be perfect. Now turn around and let me check your makeup."

Tracy had gone to the beach on her day off that week and had come back with a burn on her nose and chin. "Hmm, you're still a little red in places, but don't you like the way that new mascara accents your eyes? It makes them sparkle."

"It's fine, Mom. But it would look even better with my red tube top and jeans."

"I told you, no jeans," her mother said firmly. "Save that for the Oceanside boys. I'm sure Avery will be impressed to see how pretty you look."

"Mom, do I really have to go through with this?" Tracy asked for the hundredth time.

Before she could answer, the doorbell rang, and Nancy rushed out to answer it. Tracy stayed in the bathroom an extra minute, running a comb through her hair one last time and eyeing herself uncertainly in the mirror. Finally, resigned, she walked into the living room.

Standing in the doorway was Avery Boniface, tall and lanky and looking as if he had stepped out of the pages of an L. L. Bean catalog. From his cropped hair, navy blazer, and white cotton shirt, to his tan slacks and Topsiders, there was no doubt he was a New Englander, or at least trying to be one.

"Avery, come on in," Nancy said pleasantly, extending her hand to him.

"Thank you," Avery said politely. Tracy could see him looking around their tiny living room. Finally his eyes settled on the landscape over the fireplace. "That's really nice," he said, pointing. "Is it a Wyeth?"

"No," she answered, "it was done by a local artist."

"You have an excellent eye for talent then," he said admiringly. "You could have fooled me."

"Oh, thank you," she said, obviously impressed with his manners.

Avery reached into his pocket and handed her an envelope. "My father was sorry he couldn't see you tonight, but he sends his regards and these tickets to tomorrow's regatta."

"Thank you, Avery," Nancy cooed again. Then, remembering the purpose of Avery's visit, she turned to the hallway where Tracy stood watching them. "Oh, there you are. Come on in, honey. I'd like you to meet Avery Boniface."

"Hi, Avery," Tracy said, extending her hand.

"You must be Tracy," Avery remarked.

"That's what it says on my birth certificate," she said.

"Tracy!" her mother chided softly.

Avery chuckled. "That's all right, Mrs. Fox. I like a person with a sense of humor. Tracy must have inherited hers from you. Dad says you have one of the most entertaining talk shows on the East Coast."

Tracy stifled a groan. Who was he trying to impress? "That's right," she cut in before her mother could say anything. "My mom's the best." She turned to her mother and smiled sweetly. Two could play this game, she thought.

Glancing at his watch, Avery said, "I think we'd better be on our way, Tracy. It was nice to see you, Mrs. Fox. I hope you can come with us tomorrow."

"Of course. Nice to see you again, too. Have a good time." She watched Tracy and Avery walk out to his car.

Tracy was surprised when he opened the passenger door for her. "Please excuse the car," he said as he waited for her to get in. "It was the last one the rental place had. At least it works."

"What's the matter with it?" Tracy asked. It looked fine to her.

"With *this*?" he exclaimed, indicating the plastic dashboard. "It's junk. I've got a Porsche at home. Now that's a good car." He switched on the ignition, revving up what little engine the car had, and tore onto the road.

"One of the kids in school has a Porsche— at least his father does," Tracy commented. "I've never been in it, though. I bet it's really fast."

"Very," he said, flooring the gas pedal. When they skidded to a halt at a traffic light, he turned to her almost apologetically. "Tracy, I'd better tell you right off. I wasn't too keen on the idea of going out with you, but our parents wanted it so badly, I felt I had no choice."

He glanced over at her, for a reaction, she supposed.

"I see they teach you honesty in that prep school you go to." Tracy was surprised at how easily the words came out. But then again *she* didn't like the idea of having been forced to go out with *him*, either. "Are you always so up front with your dates?"

"I don't believe in dishonesty."

"Neither do I," Tracy retorted. The light changed, and Avery sped toward the narrow coastal road that connected the beach towns. "Speaking of which, I must admit I was impressed with the performance you put on for my mother."

"What performance?"

"Oh, come on. Do you really go around buttering up every middle-aged person you meet?"

There was no answer, and Tracy, afraid she'd gone too far, changed the subject. "By the way, where are we going?"

"I thought we'd start off the night with a good meal. Dad recommended this place."

A few minutes later, Avery pulled into the narrow road that led to the Bright Cove marina. On either side of the road were the slips at which boats were moored. And at the far end of the road, at the water's edge, was a tall building faced with weather-beaten wood. The inn was at its top.

Avery left the car with the attendant, and he and Tracy entered the restaurant. As soon as they walked in, a hostess wearing a long skirt showed them to an intimate table facing the ocean.

"Nice, isn't it?" Avery asked.

Tracy nodded. The view was not unlike the one the customers got at Captain Tony's, but in all other respects the restaurants were worlds apart. The heavy, deep blue carpeting absorbed a lot of the noise from the room, and there were bud vases and candles on each table. For the first time that night, Tracy was glad her mother had made her wear the dress.

They had been seated only a few moments when Avery flagged down their waitress. "Miss, could we have some water?" he asked importantly.

"Sure," she answered. "I'll tell the busboy."

"We'd like it now."

"I have to tell the busboy first, sir," she repeated wearily.

"I want you to get it—now," Avery insisted.

"Avery, it can wait," Tracy said quietly.

"When you two make up your mind, let me know," the waitress said and left their table.

Avery glared over at Tracy and handed her a menu. Tracy scanned it in embarrassed silence. Why was Avery so pushy? Tracy knew what it felt like to be an overworked waitress.

"Have you decided what you want to eat?" Avery asked after a few minutes. He sounded much calmer.

"I think I'll have the lobster special."

He considered that. "That sounds good," he said. "I'll have that, too." When the waitress returned with the water, Avery ordered for the two of them.

Trying to pretend that Avery didn't exist, Tracy turned toward the water and stared at the boats docked for the night, their lights along the horizon rivaling the brightness of the stars. Every now and again streams of fireworks were shot off the boat decks, adding bursts of red, blue, and white to the night sky.

"It's pretty out there, isn't it?" Avery said, trying to bring Tracy back into the room.

"Yeah," she said noncommittally.

"Look, I know you don't think much of me, and the truth of the matter is you're a little hard to take yourself. But let's try to get through this dinner, OK?"

Tracy forced a smile. "I'll try."

They waited for their lobsters in silence, looking at the view, watching the people at other tables. When the food arrived, they dug in and ate without a word. Tracy tried, but for the life of her she could not think of a way to ease the silence. She saw a look of relief cross Avery's face when the check finally arrived. He told the waitress to stay, while he whipped out his wallet and handed her several crisp ten-dollar bills. "Keep the change," he added, before getting up.

"Thank you, sir," she breathed happily.

Tracy walked back to the car with Avery, feeling slightly more kindly toward him. Even so, when he asked, "What would you like to do now?" she replied immediately, "I think I'd like to go home, if you don't mind."

She thought Avery smiled, and he made pretty good time through the clogged Fourth of July weekend traffic to Tracy's house. "Thanks for a most unusual evening," he said as he reached over to open her door.

"Thanks for the lobster. I mean it," she added as an afterthought.

"Oh, uh, Tracy," Avery said. "Could you do me a little favor?"

"What?"

"Tell your mother we had a good time. If Dad finds out the truth about tonight, he'll kill me."

Tracy raised an eyebrow. "Thought you didn't believe in dishonesty?"

Avery shrugged and spread his hands. "Whenever possible," he amended.

For the first time that evening Tracy was genuinely amused. "OK, boy scout, you can depend on me." She didn't mind stretching the truth a little. She only hoped her mother wouldn't ask her to see Avery again.

When she got inside, Tracy explained she had come home early because she had to get up for work the next day and said simply that she and Avery had had a "nice" time.

Nancy Fox went to bed that night convinced that the first stage of her summer plan for Tracy was a shining success.

Chapter Eight

Tracy woke up the following morning with a headache. She had spent half the night having second thoughts about not being truthful with her mother. As far as she was concerned, she'd be just as happy if she never saw Avery for the rest of her life, but she had a feeling she'd be going out with someone just like him the next weekend if she didn't set her mother straight.

She was hoping to catch her mother that morning and explain to her that this whole idea of fixing her up with out-of-town boys was going to be a waste of time. But her mother was still asleep by the time Tracy was ready to go to work, so she decided she'd bring the subject up after dinner that night.

The thought of having that discussion

weighed on Tracy all morning. Even though the Fourth of July breakfast crowds kept her continually hopping, she couldn't lose herself in her work.

About midway through her shift, she spotted a note waiting for her on the order clips. *Have you forgotten Waitress Rule Number One?* it said.

Tracy peered over at David, who was taking a batch of muffins out of the oven. "Hey, David, what's this about?"

He walked over to the counter and leaned against it. "Where's your smile this morning? You look like you're at a funeral."

"I feel dead this morning." She sighed.

"Too much partying last night?"

"Just the opposite," she admitted.

"Did that boy give you a hard time?"

Tracy looked stunned. "How'd you know?"

"Just a guess," he said, shrugging.

"I'm never going to see him again," Tracy added quickly, hoping he'd see what she was leading up to.

"Tracy!"

She stiffened, recognizing the nasal voice. Taking a deep breath, she turned around.

Margaret stood with her hands on her hips, an order slip clenched in her right hand. "Table twelve is waiting for menus," she said, almost shouting. "Get out there now, before I tell Mr. Parron he's got a lazy waitress on his hands!"

"Yes. Sorry," Tracy said calmly, although she was seething inside. At least when Hilda gave orders, she gave them nicely. She turned back to David to tell him she'd talk to him later, but he was already standing over the grill, laying out bacon strips.

Tracy stormed out of the kitchen, but remembering David's advice, she pasted a smile on her face as she approached the table.

The next time she went into the kitchen, she found another note waiting for her. When did David get the time to write them? This one said simply, *Margaret's an old bag. Don't let her get to you.*

Tracy answered back, *It's easier said than done, but I'll try,* although she already felt much better.

Toward the end of the shift, when things had quieted down a bit, David asked her, "How'd you make out with Margaret?"

"We've managed to stay out of each other's hair all day, thank goodness. But I think I'm ready for her now, if she tries to accuse me of falling down on the job."

"Oh, yeah?"

"Yup. I didn't make any mistakes today, and I got some decent tips from my customers. I must be doing something right. I figure if I was such a lousy waitress they'd probably stiff me, right?"

"Right," he said admiringly.

"You know, David, it's really a shame. The customers tip me just for serving the food, but you cook it and don't get anything. I don't think that's fair."

"Don't worry about me. I get my fair share. By the way, do you want some french fries? I've got half a batch here."

Tracy glanced around nervously. "Won't Parron mind?"

"No, I'd have to throw them out anyway." He shook them out of the basket and put the plate on the counter between them.

"Then I'll take one." She ate one and then another and then said, "David, are you still interested in giving me that cooking lesson?" She was amazed at how easy it was to say. But then, she felt so much more comfortable talking to David than to any other boy she knew.

"No," he said, "but I'd like to take you out sometime. How does Tuesday night sound?" He looked at her hopefully.

"It sounds great," she said. "I couldn't think of anything I'd like more."

"Neither could I," he said.

"A date?" Nancy exclaimed when Tracy told her the news that evening. "Who with?"

"A boy at work. He's—"

"A local boy?" her mother said, making it sound as if Tracy were going to date a gorilla.

"Yes," Tracy said excitedly. "I'm kind of glad he asked me today because it makes what I want to tell you that much easier. See, I think it'd be a good idea if we sort of forget about fixing me up with your friends' sons this summer."

"Wait a minute, Tracy," her mother said. "I don't know if I can do that. I'm not even sure I like the idea of this boy at all."

"How can you say that? You don't know him!" Tracy cried.

"Do you?" her mother shot back. "How much could you know? You haven't been on the job very long—you can't know much about him."

"I've been working two whole weeks. And we talk to each other every day," Tracy said. "We're friends!" She felt close to tears. What if her mother wouldn't let her go?

"Oh, Tracy, I just don't want to see you get

hurt. I'm sure he's not sophisticated enough for you."

"I don't need sophistication."

"You're too young to know what you need. Trust me on this. You'll thank me at the end of the summer for opening your eyes to what's out there in the rest of the world."

"Are you telling me I can't go out with him?" Tracy couldn't believe her mother would be so unfeeling.

Nancy Fox looked at her daughter and sighed. "Tracy, if you really want to go on this date, I'm not going to try to stop you. But I think you're wasting your time. Just keep your eyes open. Maybe the reason none of your other dates have worked out is that they've all been with local boys."

"David's not like the others, Mom. Anyway, the fact that they were locals has nothing to do with it."

"I hope you're right. But just the same, I'm not giving up my plan."

Tracy stewed for a long time. She didn't really want to date any more "sophisticates" this summer. But if things went well with David, maybe she wouldn't have to. She'd make her mother see that David was for real . . . she hoped.

Chapter Nine

Tracy stuffed her uniform into the large nylon sack she'd brought with her and strode expectantly out of Captain Tony's ladies' room. David was waiting for her in the lobby.

"You look terrific," he said, admiring the strapless green terry jumpsuit her mother had deemed unacceptable for Avery.

"Sure beats this," she said, pointing to the bag containing her uniform. "You look pretty nice yourself."

David had put on a tan-and-brown shirt over his jeans. "I had to show you there was more to my wardrobe than white shirts." He linked his arm through hers. "Shall we go?"

The sun was still high as they left the restaurant and headed in the direction of the beach town's only movie theater. The old pink

66

building was at the opposite end of the board-walk, and as they walked toward it they passed scores of sunbathers on their way home, their telltale coconut oil lingering in the air.

"See that?" said Tracy as they passed by Lloyd's Candy Shoppe. "That sign for home-made salt-water taffy?"

"Yeah."

"It's a lie. The stuff is shipped in from a factory in Camden."

"You're kidding!" said David.

"Nope. My friend Kate worked there this spring. The experience was so traumatic she had to leave town."

"Couldn't stand lying to the customers, huh?"

Tracy grinned. "Well, actually, no. She took a job at a summer camp."

"You'll probably like the movie," David said. "It's a comedy."

What a change from Avery, Tracy thought as she and David waited on line at the re-freshment stand. David seemed to enjoy her company and made her feel at ease; she didn't have to pretend to be someone else. This was even better than their short meetings at the restaurant.

But the old Tracy Fox nervousness rose to the surface soon after the theater lights

dimmed. The movie wasn't particularly funny—
a horror flick takeoff that didn't quite leave
the ground—but that had nothing to do with
her dilemma. About ten minutes into the
show, David reached out for Tracy's hand
and stroked it softly. Tracy wasn't sure how
to react. Part of her liked it, but another part
told her to pull back.

We've never been alone together, she thought.
How do I know what's on his mind? But this
is David, she argued back. He's not going to
do anything to hurt me.

Finally, she ended up letting him hold her
hand while she kept her eyes glued to the
movie, afraid to let her feelings show.

"Do you really like this movie?" David
whispered.

Tracy jumped, shocked by the suddenness
of his speech and the nearness of his lips.
"I'm thoroughly absorbed," she said, not taking her eyes off the screen.

"I don't know. I've already figured out who
the real vampire is. Have you?"

"What?" Tracy was embarrassed. Although
she'd been looking at the movie, she hadn't
been paying a bit of attention. Quickly she
reached for more popcorn so she wouldn't have
to answer.

David stroked her hand again and whispered, "I thought so. Relax, Tracy. I just want to have a good time—like you do. Don't be afraid of me."

"I'm not."

"Are you telling the truth?"

"Yes. Well . . . maybe not entirely," she admitted, turning to face him. "I'm a little nervous." She wanted everything to go just right on this date, she didn't want anything to get in the way.

"Just pretend we're back in the restaurant in our uniforms. You weren't nervous around me there."

"OK, I'll try."

Tracy felt better after they had talked about it. And then, looking closely at David, she saw a boy who looked almost as anxious about this date as she did.

Just relax and be yourself, she thought over and over, the way you were on the boardwalk.

She felt much calmer when they walked out of the theater. "Edward," she said to David when they got outside.

"No . . . David."

"No, I mean Edward was the vampire. I didn't want you to think the movie was a total waste."

He smiled. "C'mon, let's get something to eat."

"Oh, good. I'd like that."

"I'd take you to the Bright Cove Inn, but Dad wouldn't let me have the car today. How about Oceanside Manor instead?"

"David, I didn't bring nearly enough money with me," she began.

"No, dinner's my treat."

"David, that place will cost you about a week's salary."

"It'd be worth it."

"Maybe. But you don't have to take me anywhere that fancy."

"Well, I know a nice place down by the boardwalk . . . intimate, private, good food. I know the owner, too."

"Captain Tony's?" Tracy grimaced. "Forget it. I just want a nice burger with all the trimmings."

David thought a moment. "So let's go to Ernie's. They've got the best burgers in town."

"Sounds perfect!"

This time Tracy felt comfortable taking David's hand as they strolled the three blocks to Ernie's, an old storefront diner that, despite its appearance, was a popular spot, with very good food. As soon as they stepped inside, Tracy saw Mandy Delgato, a friend from school, and waved to her. Mandy grinned mischievously and flashed Tracy an I-told-you-so look. Then she whispered something to the other girl in the booth, and Tracy smiled to think she was the topic of conversation.

"Did I miss something funny?" David asked.

"No," said Tracy. "I'm just happy to be here with you. Suddenly I'm starved."

"Shouldn't be too long now," David said as they waited to be seated. "This place is really an institution. You know, I tried to get a cooking job here—that way I could have worked all year long. But there hasn't been an opening in decades. That's how I ended up with the Captain."

"You really enjoy cooking, don't you?"

"I love it. Someday I'd like to have my own restaurant."

"And be one of the great chefs of the world?"

"Sure."

"How did you get so interested in cooking, anyway?"

He took a deep breath, then said, "Can't you smell it? It's the grease. I'm addicted to it."

Tracy laughed. "No, tell me the truth. What got you into food?"

"Actually, it was survival," David said, picking up a well-worn menu. "My mother can't cook for beans." He pinched his nose in disgust.

71

"Come on, she can't be *that* bad," Tracy said.

"Oh, no? Until I was ten I thought all food came out of cans or frozen food boxes. If we'd had to depend on her to cook from scratch, we'd never have made it. But don't get me wrong. Outside of food, my mom's great."

"I guess all mothers are entitled to one fault. My mother has a one-track mind. When she gets stuck on an idea, she won't give it up. There's no arguing with her."

The waitress, a tired-looking woman in her late forties, came by to take their orders. "I'll have a pizzaburger, well done, with fries and a ginger ale," said Tracy.

"And I'll have a cheeseburger, fries, and a Coke," said David. "Make my burger rare."

As soon as the waitress left, he turned to Tracy. "How can you eat a well-done burger? It's like chomping on a hocky puck."

"The charcoal brings out the flavor of the meat. That's the only way I'll eat it."

Tracy could feel the warmth of his smile as David reached over and took her hands in his. "I may have to give you that cooking lesson after all," he said. "You've got a lot to learn about food."

Tracy turned away shyly. "David, I do know some things." She pulled back her hands, but David reached over and grabbed them again.

"Tracy, if I didn't think you were bright and interesting, would I be here with you now?"

"I figured maybe you had a soft spot for helpless females," Tracy replied, grinning facetiously.

David ignored that remark. "The first time I saw you, outside the restaurant, I knew you were special. You had this great, impish expression on your face—"

"Probably the sun in my eyes," Tracy interrupted.

"No, you looked so excited, so—"

"That was total terror."

"Hey, why do you keep interrupting me? I'm trying to say I like you."

"You are? You do?"

Their conversation was interrupted by the jarring clang of plates on the Formica tabletop. "Here you go," said the waitress, plucking some silverware from her apron pocket.

"It's a shame we've got to eat," David said, pulling back. "I like holding your hands."

"I did, too," Tracy said, taking a quick bite of her pizzaburger. "Like holding your hands, that is."

"Human touch is really important, you

73

know," David said. "I read somewhere that these scientists did all these studies with little babies, and the ones who were touched a lot were healthier and bigger. But I know from my own experience how important it is."

"You mean from all your girlfriends?" Tracy teased.

David shook his head. "To tell you the truth, there haven't been many. I meant my family. My parents are into hugging and stuff, and they passed it on to us kids."

"It must be nice to have them around. Sometimes it gets lonely being an only child."

"In our house there's no getting lonely. Whenever I'm down, all I have to do is holler, and someone will come and cheer me up."

"My mother's pretty good about that, too," Tracy said. "She knows how to make me happy—but she tends to go overboard sometimes, and she doesn't always listen to me." She wants to run my love life, she almost added.

"My mother always has your mom's show on when I come home from work," David said. He paused. "She's impressed I'm taking Nancy Fox's daughter out."

"As you can see, the saying 'like mother, like daughter' doesn't apply here."

"What do you mean?"

"Well, if you've heard her, you know she's efficient and crisp and professional. But I'm unsure of myself, and I forget things and drop things and—"

"Do you realize you're putting yourself down again?" David asked.

Tracy sighed. "I can't help it."

"I've got an idea. Give me a nickel."

"Why?" Tracy fished a coin out of her purse and handed it over.

"I'm going to break you of that nasty little trait. From now on, whenever I hear you putting yourself down, it's going to cost you a nickel. The way I figure it, either you'll wise up on yourself, or I'll make a lot of money this summer."

"Hmm. Looks like I've got no choice. With the fortune I make at work, I need all the nickels I can get."

"That will be another five cents, please."

"I wasn't knocking myself!" Tracy cried. "It's a statement of fact. No one ever said working at Captain Tony's would make you rich. But if the crowds pick up, I could make some good tips along the way."

"That's the spirit," David said. He picked up his glass. "Here's to a successful summer."

"I'll drink to that." Tracy downed the rest of her ginger ale in one gulp.

After dinner they walked back to the boardwalk. The sky was darkening quickly, but the street lamps lit the way for the steady stream of people out enjoying the evening. Most of the small souvenir shops were closed for the day, but some of the restaurants and the video parlor were still doing a brisk business.

Tracy and David bypassed this carnivallike strip in favor of the relative quiet near the bathhouse. For a while they just sat on a bench, entranced by the sound of the breaking waves.

"I could sit here for hours and never get bored," Tracy said, transfixed by the moonlight on the waves.

David took a deep breath of salt air. "I feel really lucky to live by the ocean. I'd hate ever to be too far away from it."

"Really?" Tracy turned to face him. "I feel the same way! There are lots of people right here in Oceanside who never even bother to come down here. I'll never understand that."

"They're crazy. But you know, my favorite time here is in the winter. On a calm day the waves are so low, the ocean looks like a giant, still pond." David brushed Tracy's hair from her eyes.

76

"I like it then, too, but that's because it's so quiet," she said, shifting her gaze to the ocean. "No tourists."

"I wonder why I've never seen you around before. Not too many people brave the elements that time of year." Idly he twisted a lock of her hair around his fingers.

"It's a big beach," Tracy said, wondering how to react to David's gesture. "But you and I were bound to have run into each other sooner or later."

"I'm glad it was sooner."

"Me, too."

David leaned over and kissed Tracy gently on her nose. But to her surprise, Tracy was no longer afraid. In fact, David's little touch wasn't enough to satisfy the strange emotions going on inside her. Almost by instinct, she lifted her head so that her mouth met David's. He pressed his lips on hers—for just a moment—before pulling back sharply.

"I'm sorry, Tracy. I got carried away," he apologized.

"There's nothing to be sorry for," she answered quickly, hoping he would kiss her again, hoping the kiss had meant as much to him as it had to her.

"I like you, Tracy. I've really had a good time tonight," he said, as if he knew the words she wanted to hear. Again he lowered his head and softly brushed his lips with hers. "But we'd better be getting back," he said, pulling away.

"So soon?" Tracy didn't want to go. She wanted to continue to explore these new feelings.

"I don't want to go, either. But it's getting late—and you're on early tomorrow." He rose from the bench and, taking her hand, gently pulled Tracy to her feet and out of her trance. "Don't worry. We'll have plenty of time to spend together this summer, don't you think?"

"Yes," she said hopefully. "Maybe I can even arrange to have the same day off you do," she said, surprising herself with her forwardness.

"That would be great—if we could get Parron to agree. He might put up a stink just for spite."

"I hope not," Tracy said.

Strolling happily, the two walked along Atlantic Avenue, then several blocks up Cedar Street to Tracy's house. Her mother had left the front porch light on, but the rest of the house was dark. "I guess Mom's gone out," Tracy said as she searched through her purse for her key. "I would have liked to introduce you to her."

"There'll be plenty of time for that, too," David said. As soon as she found her key, he leaned over and kissed her one last time. "Good night, Tracy."

"Good night," she said happily. "Will you be able to get home all right?"

"Sure. The buses are still running . . . though one of these days, I'm going to get Dad to lend me his car for times like this."

"Don't give up hope," she said. "And enjoy your day off."

"I'll call you tomorrow at four, OK? Good night."

"Good night," she whispered. She watched him walk down the flagstone path and all the way down Cedar until she could see him no longer.

Chapter Ten

"Tracy, is that you?"

"Mom!" Tracy cried as she approached her mother's bedroom at the back of the house. "I didn't think you were home."

"Just catching up on my reading," her mother said, taking off her half-glasses and placing them on her night table. "Tell me, how'd it go?"

"I had a wonderful time," Tracy said happily, plopping down on the edge of the bed.

Nancy bit her lip. "That's nice," she said, without much enthusiasm. Then, perking up, she added, "I've got the most wonderful news."

"What?"

"Don't make any plans for this weekend. I've got a terrific boy lined up for you."

Tracy groaned. "Oh, Mom, you didn't."

"It's all worked out. Today I got a letter from my friend Angelica. You wouldn't remember her—we worked together in New York years ago, before she married and moved to Italy. Anyway, I wrote to her three weeks ago. She and her son are taking a tour of the country this summer, and she wrote back to tell me they'll be spending this weekend here. She says she's sure her son would like to go out with you."

"This weekend?" Tracy gulped. "I don't know if I can make it."

"Why not?"

"I may have a date with David."

"Oh, dear," Nancy fretted. "He's already asked you?"

"Well, no," Tracy admitted.

"Good. Then just tell him you're busy."

Tracy began to protest, but her mother had that "don't argue with me" look on her face. "How old's her son?" she asked instead.

"Sixteen. Just like you. Angelica sent a picture of him." She rose excitedly and padded into the living room. A few moments later she handed a color snapshot to Tracy.

"He looks awfully young. Are you sure he's sixteen?"

"Of course. Angelica and I were pregnant at

the same time. It must be an old picture," she said lightly.

Actually, the boy didn't look too bad, Tracy thought. Dark, almost black hair, and thick eyebrows framing dark, somber-looking eyes. If David weren't around, she didn't think she'd mind spending an evening out with this boy. But David *was* around, and that made all the difference in the world.

"Does he speak English?"

"Giorgio? Of course he does, dear," her mother answered. "I think you'll get along with him just fine."

"That's what you said about Avery," Tracy reminded her acidly.

"I thought you liked Avery," her mother said, looking up.

"He was a snobby, pretentious creep," Tracy admitted. "I told you we had a good time as a favor to him, so he wouldn't get in trouble with his dad."

"Well, Angelica's much more down to earth than Garrett Boniface. She wouldn't raise a snob for a son. You'll see. This one you'll thank me for."

What about David? Tracy wanted to ask. But knowing it was the wrong time to bring him up, she bid her mother a hasty good night and retreated to her room. She'd try to reason with her again in the morning.

"It was so strange," Tracy said the following morning, when Jennifer asked about her date with David.

"Didn't you have a good time?" Jennifer wondered, a twinge of disappointment in her voice. She perched herself on the pink vinyl couch in the ladies' room at the restaurant, anxious to hear what had happened. The girls were on a five-minute break, their first time off that morning.

"Oh, yes!" Tracy exclaimed. "I had a wonderful time. What I meant was, it was strange just how well we got along."

"What's strange? I told you David was perfect for you."

Tracy giggled. "You were more right than you think," she said, remembering their first kiss, but she couldn't tell Jennifer about that. She looked around furtively. Neither Hilda nor Margaret was in sight. "We've got a few minutes. Do you want to hear more?"

"Do I ever! So what did you two end up doing?"

Tracy told her about the date, from beginning to end, leaving out nothing except, of course, those special kisses.

Jennifer looked puzzled. "You don't have to answer this if you don't want, but didn't he kiss you or anything?"

Tracy blushed in spite of herself. "Yes, he did." She couldn't hold back the embarrassed smile that burst upon her face.

"That's terrific!" Jennifer cried. "What did your mother say when you told her?"

"Not much. She's still committed to her 'make Tracy sophisticated' plan." Briefly she filled Jennifer in on Saturday.

"If it'll help any, I'll take Giuseppe off your hands," Jennifer offered.

"It's Giorgio. And thanks, but Mom wouldn't go for that at all. I've already tried six different ways to get out of it." Tracy recalled the brief discussion that morning in which her mother had said it was simply too late to change the plans.

"Well, keep me in mind anyhow."

Tracy couldn't help but notice the slightly wistful look on Jennifer's face. "Hey, Jen, don't worry. The summer's early. You'll find a guy, too."

"What, me worry?" Jennifer answered, shrugging. "I'll find someone. But I've got something else to tell you. Yesterday I found out there's a group in Oceanside that's trying to save buildings like the bathhouse and those wonderful old Victorian houses on Front Street."

"Gee, I didn't know that."

"It's fairly new. And small. But from what the woman I spoke to told me, they're pretty committed."

"Maybe you can meet somebody there," Tracy said.

"I'm not joining to meet boys. But then again, you never can tell." She smiled ruefully.

"Good luck," Tracy said, rising. "I think we'd better get back before Parron docks us for vacation time."

When Tracy got home late that afternoon, she found a message from David on the answering machine.

"Hi, Tracy. It's me, David. I know you're not home, but Mom's watching this soap opera, and there's a girl on it who looks just like you. Mom says you must be really pretty."

Tracy ran to the phone and called him back as soon as the message had ended.

"So 'a day without Tracy is a day without sunshine'?" she chirped, repeating the last part of his message. "Give me a break."

"OK, so it's a little trite. But I found myself looking at my watch every other minute, thinking, well, it's twelve o'clock, Tracy must be balancing five plates on her tray while listening to Parron shout in her right ear and Hilda yell in her left ear, with Margaret blocking the way."

"Not quite," she said. "At twelve, I was patiently reciting the entire menu to a table full of sweet little old ladies. And I didn't hear a peep out of Parron all day."

David laughed. "I knew you'd win over that stone heart sooner or later."

"Actually, it's Margaret I'd like to strangle. This morning I helped her out at a couple of tables and didn't get so much as a 'thank you'!"

"She's jealous, Tracy."

"Of me?" she exclaimed, puzzled.

"Sure," David said. "Here you are, young, pretty, full of life—and the best she can come up with is Parron."

"I never thought of it that way," she said. "But it makes sense, I think."

"I forgot to add the part about your having a wise and charming boyfriend."

"Do I?" asked Tracy lightly. "I didn't know that one date made you my boyfriend."

"Well, I plan to do something about that. I've got to help my dad with some things tonight, but I'd like to see you before work tomorrow."

"When?" Tracy wondered. "Four in the morning?"

"Something like that."

"David, that's crazy! Nobody's up at that hour."

"The fish are. I want you to go fishing with me."

Tracy sighed. "But at *four*?"

"All right, four-thirty, at the beach. That'll give us a few hours before I go to work. Are you game?"

"Sure," she answered, with just the slightest hesitation. Four in the morning! "I'll be there."

As soon as she hung up the phone, she set her alarm clock and hoped her fuzzy brain would remember why she was getting up at that ghastly hour on her day off.

Of course, there was still the matter of getting permission from her mother. Tracy decided to raise the subject at dinner, but Nancy spent the whole meal raving about how well her remote broadcast at the beach had gone that day.

Tracy didn't want to spoil her mother's triumph with her news, so she decided to put it off until after she'd done the dishes. But when she got out of the kitchen, her mother was on the phone, and Tracy wasn't about to interrupt her, so she went to her room and started a letter to Kate. She had just finished describing her date with David when her mother knocked on the door. "Did you want to talk to me, Tracy?"

Tracy put the notepaper down. "Yeah. Mom, you know how you've been saying all summer that I should expose myself to new experiences?"

"Of course. I've been wondering if you've really heard me."

"I have," she said. "And if someone asked me to take part in a new experience, you wouldn't have any objections, right?"

"Well, there are some experiences I have a feeling you're not ready for. What are we talking about?"

"Fishing," Tracy said simply.

"Fishing?" her mother echoed. She shrugged. "I suppose I don't have any objections to that."

"Thanks, Mom." Tracy got up and gave her mother a big hug.

"I didn't know it meant that much to you. Who are you going with?"

"David," Tracy answered.

"That boy? Now, *Tracy*—"

"Oh, come on, Mom, I can still go, can't I?"

"Yes," her mother answered. "But I'm liking the idea less and less."

"Why? David's a really nice guy."

"He may be nice, dear, but that's not the point. He just doesn't fit into my plans for you this summer. With your friends all away and your taking on a new job, I think this is a good time to introduce you to different types of people. I'm sure David's a fine boy, but he's just a *local* boy, someone you could date any other time of the year."

"So? What about what *I* want?"

"You're too young to know what you want," her mother said, repeating the old refrain.

Nancy went on to complain about the boys who sometimes hung around her broadcast booth, saying how ordinary they were and that she didn't want her daughter dating ordinary, uninteresting boys. Tracy tried to tell her mother that David was anything but ordinary, and very smart, but it was as if her mother had already closed her mind and Tracy could do nothing to open it.

As Tracy got ready for bed that night, she realized that all the talk in the world wouldn't convince her mother of David's worth. She'd have to *show* her he was better than any city boy her mother could come up with. She didn't know how she was going to do it, but she'd find a way.

Chapter Eleven

Somehow Tracy managed to meet David at the beach promptly at four-thirty. Her eyes were open enough to spot him down at the jetty, with two poles in his hands and a tackle box and ice chest at his feet. Taking off her shoes and rolling up her jeans, she jogged slowly across the cool, moist sand.

"You know, you can get arrested for forcing a girl out of bed this early in the morning."

"Good morning to you, too," he said, kissing her on the forehead. "Trust me, this will be fun. See, we're not the only ones out here." He pointed to three men at the far end of the jetty, their poles already set in place.

"I had a bit of a hard time getting out this morning. My mom thought I was crazy."

"I guess she's not much on fishing. Anyway, I'm glad you made it."

"Just tell me one thing. What's the point of this?"

"To catch fish, of course. Some blues, maybe some flounder. Besides, I thought it'd be fun to watch the sunrise together."

"That's still about an hour and a half away." She shivered under her navy blue slicker. "Where's my pole?"

"Hey, not so fast. I've got to bait us up, first." Kneeling down, David opened the tackle box and took out a container of mussels. "Once I get these things in the water, the fish will come running."

Tracy was impressed with how quickly David attached the bait to the hooks. "Do you do this often?" she asked.

"Maybe five or six times a year. My dad used to take me more often when I was younger. Once in a while we'd go on one of those all-day charters and come home with all sorts of fish."

"Did you have to clean them?" Tracy asked.

"Yeah," David said. "Still do. But it's not so bad if you have a good sharp knife and know what you're doing."

"You are a glutton for punishment," Tracy

said, taking one of the poles. "No wonder you like me."

"Five cents, please," David said quickly.

"And wide awake, too." She stuck her hands in her jacket pockets. "I didn't bring any money with me."

"You're good for it," David said. "I'll put it on your tab." Taking Tracy's hand, he led her to the edge of the jetty, a few feet away from the other fishermen. "You ever handle one of these before?"

Tracy shook her head.

"Let me show you how. Just release the tension on the reel and gently cast it into the water, like this." Tracy could hear the line plop into the water below them. "Now you do it."

Holding the pole with both hands, Tracy followed David's instructions and released her line, but it tangled up in itself. "Oh, Fill—" she began to exclaim and then stopped. Getting mad at herself wasn't going to solve anything. Taking a deep breath, she put down the pole and attended to her line.

"Hey, it's all right," David said as he helped her unsnag it. "These things happen all the time. It's just a matter of getting used to it." He handed the pole back to Tracy. "Try again."

"This time it's going in." And it did. The

line had been in the water no more than a minute when she said, "OK, David, where are my fish?"

"Patience, Tracy. Fishing demands patience. Now, let's rest our poles between the rocks and relax. Look out over there." He pointed to the ocean. "You can see the sun starting to peek through in the middle of the Atlantic. Won't be long to sunrise now."

Tracy sighed. "It *is* sort of pretty this time of day . . . in a moody sort of way."

David patted her shoulder. "I knew you'd like it once you gave it a try."

"I didn't say anything about fishing. So far, that's pretty boring." She leaned over the water and called out, "Hey, fish, come on, wake up. Breakfast's here." The three fishermen glared over at her.

"Shhh." David pulled Tracy back and brought her close. "You've got to be quiet, or you'll scare off the fish."

"Sorry." She examined her pole for signs of life. Nothing. "Did I just ruin the entire morning?"

"I don't think so," David whispered. "But you've got to give them time."

Tracy rested her head on his shoulder, letting the steady sea breeze wash across her face. "The boardwalk looks so eerie," she commented. "Like a ghost town."

"That's what I like about coming down here so early. You can see everything come to life. Just wait, around six or so the joggers will start to come out, then the bicycle riders and the dog walkers, and finally the early sun freaks. I kind of like it the way it is right now. I feel like the whole place belongs to me . . . to us."

"Don't forget those fishermen. They might feel neglected."

"All right. They can have everything to the south, and I'll take everything to the north. Think that's fair?"

"Shall I ask them?"

Wrapping her in his arms, David said, "No. I have something else in mind." He lowered his head to hers and kissed her gently.

"Now that's the kind of wake-up call I like."

"Well, if that's—" His attention was suddenly diverted. "Tracy, your line! It's moving."

"What do I do?" she asked frantically.

"Here, I'll show you." David took hold of the pole and slowly reeled in the line. On the end was a nearly foot-long bluefish flapping its tail. David unhooked it and put it in the ice chest.

"Your first fish, Tracy. What do you think?"

"You did all the work," she said. "The compliments are yours."

"Well—oh, there's another one." David's line was jerking wildly, and he quickly moved over and went to work on it. This fish was a little feistier, and it took him several minutes to bring it in.

"Good work," Tracy said, patting him on the back. "What are you going to do with them?"

"Eat them. What else?" David said as he rebaited the lines. "I thought I'd try out a new fish recipe I saw in the *Times*. Would you care to join me?"

"As co-fisherperson, I think I'm entitled."

"Deal," David said. "How's Saturday night?"

"Oh, David, I'd love to . . . but I can't. My mom's having company, and I've got to stick around and play hostess." She felt more comfortable telling him this lie than admitting the truth about Giorgio.

"That's too bad." David sounded disappointed. "But if you've got to, you've got to. Is there anything I can do to change your mind?"

"Believe me, if it was up to me, there'd be no question. But the decision is out of my hands."

The two sat back on the jetty and watched their lines bob in the water. The sun was just starting to rise, casting a long, golden streak over the horizon. Tracy watched as the sparkling rays of light on the water slowly began to creep in her direction.

"It's going to be a hot day," she said. "No clouds."

"That'll mean plenty of business—and a hot kitchen."

"Ugh, don't think of work right now. Let's enjoy this moment."

But too soon afterward it was time for them to pack up their things, David to head to the restaurant, and Tracy to take the rest of her day off. Back in her bed that morning, Tracy reflected on how much she had enjoyed the fishing trip. She might even do it again, she thought, though next time she'd prefer it if David took her night fishing.

Chapter Twelve

"Can I die now?" Tracy asked her mother when she limped through the front door that Saturday afternoon.

"Poor Tracy." Nancy Fox took her daughter in her arms. "What happened?"

"It wasn't enough that nearly everyone on the Eastern Seaboard decided to descend on Captain Tony's for the day, but Parron also booked four busloads for lunch. At twelve o'clock there was a line that stretched all the way to Front Street!"

"It sounds like it was even busier than the Fourth."

"It was! I never made so many trips back and forth to the kitchen. My feet are killing me!" She fell onto the sofa.

"Go soak them," her mother suggested.

"You've got a couple of hours before Giorgio will be here."

"Can't you tell him I've got a previous engagement—with my bed?"

"Tracy, you know how much this means to me."

"All right, I'll be ready in time," Tracy said, heading toward the bathroom.

She sat in the bathtub for half an hour, letting the tension of the day escape. Wistfully, she recalled the concerned look on David's face when he'd wished her a good time with her company. She felt bad now about deceiving him, but at the same time, she thought it would be better for David this way, a case of what he didn't know not hurting him.

"You'll really like Giorgio," her mother said as Tracy got dressed. She had decided on her blue harem pants and matching blouse, one of the most comfortable outfits she owned.

"Have you met him?" she asked, brushing her hair.

"No, not yet. But I had lunch with his mother today. She couldn't stop talking about him. He sounds like a dear."

"Terrific," Tracy said deadpan, reaching for her lip gloss. "I can't wait."

"Now don't do that to me, Tracy. Why can't you try to have a good time?"

"What if he hates America?" she asked.

"I decided to make it easy on you and bought two tickets to Great Adventure. Even if you don't like him, you'll enjoy the rides."

Her mother looked so hopeful that Tracy felt a little ashamed. "It was nice of you to think of giving us something to do. I'll really try to have a good time. Honest." She gave her mother a quick hug.

"That's him!" her mother cried as the doorbell rang. She hurried out of Tracy's room to answer it. Tracy followed, lagging behind.

"Angelica!" Her mother greeted her friend warmly. "Oh, and this must be Giorgio."

Tracy glimpsed the boy from the photograph. He was dark-haired and cute, but he still looked young. He stood slightly behind his glamorous mother.

Bowing politely, he said softly, "*Buona sera,* Mrs. Fox."

"Giorgio, this is my daughter, Tracy."

"Hi, Giorgio," said Tracy, moving forward to shake his hand. "Nice to meet you."

Giorgio smiled shyly.

"I thought I'd drive you there," said Tracy's mother. "Are you ready to go now?"

Tracy spent an uncomfortable thirty minutes in the backseat with Giorgio, not knowing what to say. But then, Giorgio didn't say anything, either. Meanwhile, their mothers talked nonstop. Tracy was awfully relieved when her mother dropped them off at the entrance to the park, thinking they'd both be happier once they got on the rides. "I'll be back at eleven," Nancy told Tracy.

"We'll be here," she answered. "Thanks for driving us."

Alone now with Giorgio, Tracy felt even more uncertain. "Shall we go in?" she said at last.

"Yes," he said, slowly taking in the surroundings.

Tracy guided him to the line of people outside the gate. "So how do you like America?" she asked, fumbling for something to say.

"It is nice," he answered. "Very big."

"What have you seen?"

"We've been to New York City and now to here. Later, we will leave for California."

"How nice. I've never been to California," she said.

They went through the gate and onto the midway filled with shops and attractions. "What do you want to do first?" she asked.

"Whatever you want," he said, wide-eyed. "There's so much here."

"How about the roller coasters? Let's go on all of them, OK?" Without waiting for a response, Tracy headed in the direction of the nearest ride, Giorgio following.

"Just as I figured. A long line," Tracy pointed out as they neared the giant roller coaster.

Tracy tried to keep up small talk during their half-hour wait, but Giorgio was very quiet. Finally they reached the front of the line. Happily, Tracy hopped into the front seat of the first car. Giorgio followed reluctantly. Once they were strapped in their seats, he held on to the safety bar for dear life.

"Hey, Giorgio, the ride hasn't started yet," Tracy said, stretching out her legs and arms. "It's going to be fun. Watch."

Seconds later the car started its gradual ascent to the stars.

"Isn't it fun, Giorgio?" she shouted over the din of people and moving machinery.

His answer was a muted shout, which was lost on Tracy as the coaster entered a series of quick back-and-forth turns. Then it rose again to an even higher point. Again, Tracy held up her arms in glee, while Giorgio sat with his eyes closed.

A scant two minutes later, the ride was over. "You can open them now, Giorgio," Tracy said, rising from her seat. "We're through."

Red-faced, he climbed out of the car.

"Where to now?" Tracy wondered.

"I think I need to sit down," Giorgio said.

Tracy led him to a small concrete bench across from a refreshment stand. "Do you mind if I go over to that stand? I'm thirsty."

Tracy bought sodas for the two of them and carried them over to the bench.

"I'm sorry, Giorgio," Tracy said with concern. "Maybe the amusement park wasn't a very good idea."

But Giorgio wouldn't give up. "No, I'm having a nice time, Tracy," he said. "I'm ready for another ride."

"Well, maybe we ought to try something a little less strenuous. Like the Ferris wheel."

They walked over to the big wheel and got on. "This is better, isn't it?" Tracy asked as the ride began and they crept leisurely up toward the night sky. "Look, you can see the whole park from up here."

"It is better," Giorgio admitted. "Much better." Then without warning, he leaned over and kissed Tracy.

"Giorgio!" she cried, pulling away.

"It is in gratitude—" he began.

"Gratitude, my—" Tracy stopped herself. "I don't know how you do it in Italy, but in America you—you take your time."

"I'm sorry." Giorgio retreated to his side of the seat.

Tracy was glad when the ride was over. They went on a number of other rides, but Tracy was careful to avoid the other roller coasters. Giorgio was grim-faced throughout the evening and seemed bothered by the crowds.

Checking her watch at one point, Tracy saw it was almost ten-thirty. Just another half hour to endure, she consoled herself.

"We're going to have time for just one more ride. Let's make it the log flume."

"More crowds?" asked Giorgio.

"Afraid so."

"Then let's just go see if your mother's here," he said tiredly.

Tracy glanced at her watch. "Are you sure?"

"More than sure," he insisted. "Let's go."

So for half an hour the two of them stood mutely at the front entrance waiting for Nancy Fox to arrive. Tracy wasn't sure which of them was more relieved when she came.

"I still don't understand it," Tracy's mother said the following night at dinner, passing Dina the salad bowl. "Angelica couldn't stop bragging about what a wonderful boy he is."

"Boy is the key, Mom," Tracy said, putting down her fried chicken. "I can't believe he's sixteen—he acted like he was six."

104

"You're exaggerating, Tracy."

"You wouldn't say that if you'd been there. He acted scared."

"But he's new to the country. Maybe he was overwhelmed."

"Don't they have people in Italy?" Tracy wanted to know. "He was spooked by the crowds. Hardly what I'd call sophisticated, Mom."

"Well—"

"Not every boy is going to be to Tracy's liking," Dina pointed out. "I understand she has a new boyfriend."

"David? That's his name, honey, isn't it? Yes, a boy from work. Ah, well. . . . But we still have to find a *proper* boy for you this summer."

"What's wrong with David?"

"We've gone through this before, dear. I'm sure there's nothing wrong with him, but he *is* a local. I just know we can do better, you'll see."

Tracy looked at her mother in despair. How could she ever convince her that David was the boy she really wanted?

Chapter Thirteen

Two nights later, Tracy went to David's house for dinner. She dressed carefully, as it was the first time she would meet his family. She had to make a good impression. After deliberating for what seemed like hours, she chose her beige sundress with the matching jacket. It was a subdued, but sophisticated, outfit.

At six-thirty, she knocked on the door of the Saylors' modest Cape Cod house. "You must be Tracy," said the girl who answered.

"And you're Alice?" Tracy smiled at the skinny, freckle-faced girl.

Alice grinned impishly. "How'd you know?" Then, turning around she shouted, "David, Tracy's here!"

"Hey, the whole neighborhood will know," David said, wiping his hands on a towel as he approached. He kissed Tracy on the nose. Alice giggled.

"Something smells good," said Tracy.

"Well, you missed out on those fish we caught, so I had to go out and buy some more. But believe me, it was worth it."

"I can't wait."

"First, I want you to meet my parents." David led her through the tiny living room to the den, where his parents were watching television. His father rose upon seeing Tracy.

"I thought I heard the door." He smiled and extended his hand. "Welcome, Tracy. It's a pleasure to meet you."

"You're as lovely as David said you were," said his mother. "As you can see, my son doesn't allow me in the kitchen when he's preparing a meal."

"Yeah, that's 'cause she can't cook," came the scowling reply of a tow-headed boy still glued to the television.

"Billy, that's no way to talk about your mother," scolded his father.

"So, David tells us that Nancy Fox is your mother," Mrs. Saylor said, beaming. "I listen to her all the time. She's marvelous. Where does she come up with all those unusual people?"

107

"She seems to have a way of attracting them," said Tracy. "She's sort of unusual herself." She hoped Mrs. Saylor wouldn't dwell on the topic of her mother. Tracy knew her mother didn't want her to be at David's house in the first place.

"I've got to get back to the kitchen," David said. "Ma, why don't you entertain Tracy until dinner's ready?"

"Can't I help you, David?" Tracy asked.

"My kitchen is off limits to everyone—even you," he added. "Dinner should be ready in about ten minutes, though, so I won't be long." Flinging his towel over his shoulder, he headed back to the kitchen.

"Let me show you the rest of the house," Mrs. Saylor said. Quickly she gave Tracy a tour. The house was neat but cramped, filled with mementos and children's artwork. The tour ended in the backyard, where she showed Tracy her vegetable garden.

"This is really neat," Tracy said, eyeing row after row of peas and beans and ripening tomatoes. "You grow all these things by yourself? My mom and I have trouble keeping the lawn green."

"It's not so difficult," Mrs. Saylor said. "It just takes time and a little tender loving care. I grow them, and David cooks them."

"You must enjoy having David cook for you."

"Oh, yes," Mrs. Saylor agreed. "My mother was wonderful in the kitchen, but whatever talents she had, skipped a generation and landed on David. But tell me about yourself. How do you like working at the restaurant?"

"I like it," Tracy answered. "I really do. It's a lot of hard work, and the hours are long, but I meet interesting people. Just this morning I had a customer who won five thousand dollars in Atlantic City."

"Must have left you a big tip," Mr. Saylor commented as he joined them in the garden.

"That was the interesting thing," Tracy explained. "He stiffed me."

"What a shame," Mrs. Saylor said. She looked up suddenly as she heard a bell ringing.

"Dinner is served," David called from the kitchen.

Mrs. Saylor seated Tracy in the chair next to David's and then went into the kitchen to help serve the meal. First came a huge salad, then buttered potatoes and sauteed green beans, all fresh from the garden, followed by the main course.

"*Voilà!*" David carried the platter to the table. "Sea bass almondine à la David!" He removed the cover, revealing a large broiled fish smothered in almonds, mushrooms, and a light sauce.

"Oh, David, it smells heavenly," breathed Tracy.

David retreated to the kitchen and came back with a smaller plate. "Don't worry, brother and sister, I haven't forgotten about you." He placed a platter of plain broiled fish between them.

"Aren't you going to have some of this?" Tracy asked, pointing to the bass.

"With all that gunk on it?" said Billy. Alice giggled.

Tracy thoroughly enjoyed the meal. Not only was David's food delicious, but the Saylors were so friendly, she lost whatever nervousness she'd had at first. Between bites of the fish, she talked about herself, her work, her hopes of winning a scholarship to college.

"Do you want to follow in your mother's footsteps?" Mrs. Saylor asked.

"Oh, no. She's one of a kind," Tracy said. "I'll probably end up in business or finance, maybe being a banker or a corporate executive, something more cut-and-dried than radio."

"I admire your ambition," Mr. Saylor said.

"David kissed her," Alice spoke up just then. "A big, large, mushy kiss."

"David?" his father questioned him. "In front of your sister?"

"It was just a brush on the nose, Dad. You know how Alice likes to exaggerate." He reached across the table and ruffled his sister's hair, which sent Alice into another fit of giggles.

Later, when Tracy volunteered to help David wash the dishes, he kidded her. "Since when have you decided to become a banker?"

"Since about a half-hour ago. It just seemed like the right thing to say. I wanted to make a good impression. Anyway, you never know."

"I think you've done just fine." He smiled. "By the way, when am I going to get a chance to work my cooking magic on your mother?"

"Soon, I hope. She's been really busy at the station, you know, preparing for those live remotes she's doing at the beach. Did I tell you Jennifer's going to be on one of her shows?"

"No. Why?"

"I told Mom about that preservation group Jennifer joined, and she lit up like a Christmas tree. She's going to give the group a lot of time on her show."

"That's wonderful."

"It's funny, though, how Jennifer's opened

me up to what she likes to call 'Oceanside's hidden treasures.' "

David looked at Tracy tenderly. "We can all be blind to things until someone else opens our eyes. That's nothing to be ashamed about—it's part of growing-up."

"You're very philosophical tonight," Tracy said.

"I am? I take it back, then. Can't be too serious—especially when I meet your mother. I'm going to be nothing but a storehouse of jokes."

"Spare me. Knowing you, they're likely to be as corny as your mother's vegetable garden." She reached into the dishwater and flicked a few drops of water at him.

"Oooh," cried David. "This is war. She can dish it out, let's see if she can take it." He cupped some water in his hands and threw it at her.

Tracy shrieked and retaliated by taking a glass of grape juice and holding it over David's head.

He grabbed it before she could dump it on him. "Enough," he said, putting the glass in the sink. "I have a better idea." He wrapped his arms around Tracy's waist and kissed her tenderly.

"What if Alice sees us?" she asked after their lips parted.

"We may traumatize her for life, I guess. I never said I was the perfect brother."

Chapter Fourteen

"Tracy, I'm glad I caught you," her mother said as she entered the kitchen the following morning.

"I've got only a few minutes," Tracy said, finishing her toast. "I made some coffee. Want some?"

"Please. My eyes are still closed." Nancy plopped into a chair.

Tracy poured the coffee as her mother continued. "How would you like to see The Unispace?"

"The who?"

"Not The Who. The Unispace. They're playing at the auditorium this weekend. I thought all you kids liked that kind of music."

"Oh, I remember now," she said, scrunchng up her nose. "They're wild, I think, although I've never heard any of their stuff."

"Would you like to see them?" her mother asked expectantly.

"Not particularly."

"Oh," said her mother, a little too casually. "One of my guests this week has written a book on rock music. He told me he'd be bringing his son down with him because he's a big fan of the group and—"

"Mom, you didn't!" Tracy wailed.

"Now, hear me out," her mother said.

"I don't have to. You've fixed me up with this guy's son, haven't you?"

"Well, yes—"

"Well, I'm not going!" Tracy said defiantly.

"Tracy!"

"Mom, I told you after that thing with Giorgio, I'm not interested in being set up on another of your blind dates. I've got a boyfriend I'm perfectly happy with."

"A perfectly boring boy."

"You haven't *met* David. How can you say that? You didn't even ask if I had a good time last night!"

"Shhh, not so early in the morning. Quiet down. I forgot about your date. I'm sorry. Nevertheless, I am your mother, and I am older than you, so I know a little more about life. You're only sixteen. I've been guilty of sheltering you all these years, and now I think it's time you saw what the rest of the world is like."

"But what about David?" Tracy asked.

"What about him?" her mother wanted to know. "You two aren't going steady or anything."

"Well, no, not really . . ." Tracy began.

"So what's the problem?"

Tracy didn't know how to answer that. True, she wasn't officially dating only David, but if things continued to go the way they were, she'd certainly like to be. Only she didn't think her mother could understand that. "If I go out with this guy, Mom, will you promise this will be the last time you fix me up with someone?"

"It really bothers you that much?"

"It really does."

Nancy looked at her daughter for a long time, lips pursed, frowning slightly. Finally she said, "All right, dear. This is the last one."

"Thanks, Mom," Tracy said.

Now all she had to do was figure out a way to tell David.

Tracy stormed into Captain Tony's in a foul mood. She was glad to see the end of her nother's fix-ups, but she hated the way her nother had pushed her into this last date, and she hated herself for not having the guts to stand up and defy her.

"Looks like you got up on the wrong side of the bed this morning," Jennifer commented as soon as she walked in.

"It shows that much?"

"Yeah. What happened? Didn't you have a good time at David's?"

"That was terrific, but right now it seems like a thousand years ago. My mom dropped another bombshell this morning."

"Another date?"

Tracy nodded. "I know she means well, but she's being so pushy about it, like I'm incapable of making my own decisions. At least I got her to agree not to put me through this anymore."

"Well, that's really something! And maybe this one will be an improvement."

"Could anyone be worse than the last one?" Looking around then, Tracy spotted a couple at one of her tables. "The first round has begun. We'll talk more later."

But Tracy didn't get a chance to stop all morning. David, too, was so busy he didn't even have time to look at her.

By contrast, lunch was a breeze. The day

117

was beautiful and mild, and anyone with sense was out enjoying the sun and ocean. When Tracy placed her first lunch order, she found a note waiting for her. *You were a hit. Mom wants to know if you'd like to come to dinner again Saturday night.*

Tracy's heart sank. Why Saturday, of all nights! She debated over the answer and finally wrote: *Would love to come back, but Saturday is out.*

When she went back to the kitchen a few minutes later, she found another note that said simply: *Why?*

"David," Tracy whispered through the divider. "We'll talk later, OK?"

When Tracy reappeared in the dining room, she found Mrs. Logan seated at one of her tables. The older woman looked distraught. "What's the matter?" Tracy asked.

"You look like the one who's troubled, Tracy. If you don't mind my butting into your affairs, would you tell me what's wrong?"

Tracy sighed. "I'm having an awful time hiding my feelings today." Briefly she recapped the situation with her mother and David and this weekend's mystery boy.

"My, my, the troubles of a teenager," Mrs. Logan mused, giving her a little smile.

"It's not funny, Mrs. Logan."

"Of course not, dear," she said, "but it's not as dire a situation as you think, either. This David seems like an understanding boy. Why don't you tell him the truth?"

"I can't do that. It'd hurt him."

"Tracy, I've told a few fibs in my day—and I've regretted every one of them. You're always better off with the truth, believe me."

"I'd like to, Mrs. Logan."

The older woman put down her spoon. "Try it and see what happens."

Tracy thought about what Mrs. Logan had to say, finally concluding that anyone who managed to reach her age without being grumpy all the time had to know something about human nature. She decided to take her suggestion.

After work Tracy met David in front of the Video Shack. "About Saturday night—" she began.

"Yeah, what's up?"

"Well, I'm, uh, going to be sort of busy," she hedged.

"Doing what?"

"I've got another date," she said in a low voice.

"You *what*?"

"It was prearranged by my mother. Just like the others. I had nothing to do with it."

"What others?" David asked sharply. "What are you talking about?"

"You know." She forced a smile. "The other boys I was fixed up with."

"No, I don't know." David's face was red with anger.

Tracy was beginning to think telling the truth wasn't such a good idea, but she'd gone this far already and couldn't stop now. "They were friends of my mother's. I went out with the first one the night I had to postpone our first date. The second date was the night I told you I was entertaining with my mother."

"You lied to me, Tracy. I don't believe it," David said. As if he didn't really want to know the answer, he asked, "What about this guy?"

"I don't want to see him," Tracy insisted.

"So get out of it!" David said, his voice rising.

"I'd like to, but he was handed to me as— what is it?—a *fait accompli.*"

David ignored that. "How can you do this? I thought you were happy with me."

"I am, David," she said earnestly. "Believe me, I like you."

"Then break the date."

"I can't."

"Look, Tracy, I like you a lot, too. But I

120

have this funny thing—I don't like the idea of my girl going out with someone else."

"Maybe you can go out with someone, too. We never said we were tied to each other or anything." Tracy regretted the words as soon as she said them.

"I don't want to go out with anyone else!" he shouted. "I want you, Tracy Fox. But I don't want you part-time. Either you break this date, or don't count on dating me again."

"David, you can't mean that!"

"There are few things I stick to my convictions on, and this is one of them. I'm sorry, Tracy. You'd better think hard about it." He walked off.

"David!" Tracy called after him. "What about our date tonight?"

But David didn't turn around, and Tracy didn't want the humiliation of running after him.

By Friday an uneasy truce had settled between them. Tracy held off giving David an answer until the last possible second. All week long she hoped that Keith, the boy she was due to date on Saturday, would break a leg or discover he was allergic to the ocean, *anything* so she could get out of their date. But by Friday she realized nothing of the sort would happen. So she resigned herself to taking her chances with David, sure that when it came right down to it, she could convince him this date would change nothing in their relationship.

"I'm sorry, Tracy, I'm not buying it," David told her that afternoon after she had made her plea. "I really liked you, too. A lot."

"David, it's just one night. It doesn't mean anything to me," she cried. "I can't get out of it. Don't you understand that?"

"No, I don't, Tracy. Call me dumb or hardheaded or whatever, but I just can't handle it."

For hours Tracy replayed that scene in her head, concluding she was in a no-win situation. "Keith," she said before she went to bed that night, "you'd better be worth it."

Chapter Fifteen

"Hello . . . Keith?"

Openmouthed, Tracy stood at the door facing her date for the evening. She didn't know whether to laugh or to cry—all she knew was if her mother had gotten a look at this kid beforehand, she never would have given her approval. Dressed in a black sleeveless T-shirt and tight, black pants, Keith was anything but her mother's picture of a sophisticated boy.

"Come on in, Keith. I'm Tracy."

"Hey, Trace. Call me Sting. I don't answer to Keith."

"Sting? You mean like that guy from the Police?"

"You got it."

Tracy was thinking, I got dressed up for this?

Tracy's mother entered the foyer. "Oh, you must be Keith. Your father told me all about you." Her blank face masked her reaction to the strange-looking boy.

"Did he tell you he likes to be called Sting?" Tracy asked tartly. She turned back to him. "I guess we'd better go. Ready, Sting?"

"Sure."

The Unispace were playing at the Ocean-side Auditorium, a small arena that booked concerts during the busy summer season. Tracy was too stunned to say anything during the short ride over. It didn't matter—she didn't have to. Sting kept up a running commentary about the Unispace while he drove.

"They are the greatest, babe," he said.

"Don't call me babe," Tracy said crossly. "My name is Tracy."

"Sure thing. Tracy." Pulling into the parking lot next to the auditorium, Sting turned to her. "Listen, I'm glad you could make it tonight. I know these arrangements can be a drag. But don't let it get to you. You'll have a good time. The Unispace are terrific."

Tracy and Sting made their way toward the concert hall, where a line was already forming at the entrance.

"I hadn't realized the Unispace were so popular," she said, gazing at the impatient crowd surrounding them. Obviously, a lot of people liked the Unispace enough to travel to this little town to see them.

"Yeah, this is one of their few shows in the area. I saw them at the Garden last winter."

"You see a lot of concerts in New York?"

"Pretty many."

"I don't get up there too often. When I do, it's mostly to go shopping, check out the museums, stuff like that."

"Boring," he said, looking straight ahead. "Hey, the doors are opening. Let's go."

It didn't take them long to find their seats, which, as Tracy had figured, were near the front. She eyed her surroundings with a curious detachment. She didn't care much for concerts and wished she were anyplace else. Like anyplace with David. But that, she was beginning to realize with painful reality, might never happen again. He hadn't said a word to her all day long. Tracy hated him for being so stubborn. Still, she wondered what he was doing right then.

Her thoughts were interrupted by Sting. "I'm hungry. Want anything?"

"A soda would be fine."

Sting returned a few minutes later. "I got you a dog, too. Thought you might be hungry."

"Thanks," she said. "Funny, working in a

restaurant all day, I hardly ever get a chance to eat."

They ate in silence. Then Tracy said, "I forgot to ask you. Who's the opening act?"

"No one. The Unispace always work alone. They don't like anyone upstaging them." Looking up at the mass of amplifiers, musical instruments, and people before them, he added, "Looks like they're almost ready to go. Who-ya!" He slapped his hands together, then raised a fist in the air.

The music seemed to be having an effect on him, Tracy noticed. He was beginning to look at her in a strange way, a way she didn't like.

"Excuse me, I've got to go to the bathroom." She squeezed down the aisle and up to the back of the arena.

The line for the ladies' room was horrendous, stretching nearly the length of the auditorium. About five minutes passed, and the line seemed hardly to have moved. At least the wait gave her time to think.

Just as she reached the door, the sounds of strident guitar riffs filled the air. To her surprise, Tracy found the music infectious and, like the other girls on line, began to move with the beat.

At last she reached the rest room. The music

was just as loud in there, but Tracy decided she preferred to stay there for the time being rather than return to Sting. She stood in front of one of the old mirrors and though she could hardly see herself, took out her comb and ran it through her hair. Finally, bored with looking at her reflection, she decided to go back to her seat. She had toyed briefly with the idea of simply going home, but some crazy curiosity made her want to see this date through to the bitter end.

At last she returned to her seat. Sting was gone. Puzzled, Tracy peered around the haze, finally spotting him on the aisle, dancing wildly to the music. Just then he turned and caught her eye. Sting smiled blankly and returned his attention to the group. He had hardly missed her at all, Tracy thought, puzzled by his behavior. For the rest of the concert she stayed in her seat, glad she didn't have to put up with him.

"That was a great concert," Tracy told him afterward when he rejoined her. "They're a lot better than I thought."

"I knew you'd like them, babe."

"Would you stop calling me babe?" she said with irritation.

"All the girls like it."

"Not *this* one," she emphasized.

"Hey, lighten up," he whispered. "We've got a whole night ahead of us."

"No, I've got to go home now. My mother's expecting me."

"A real mama's girl, huh." He snorted. "Well, all right. I'm not going to twist your arm or anything. You want to go home now, I'll take you."

"Thanks, Sting." Tracy brightened. At least he had *some* sense of honor.

Very soon Tracy was safely at home, and Sting was a memory she hoped she could soon forget.

But she lay awake all night with a boy on her mind. David. After Sting, Tracy once again felt how lucky she was to have found a person who liked her and respected her for herself. Boy, what a summer this was turning out to be. Everything was mixed up. Somehow she had to figure out a way to make David talk to her again.

Chapter Sixteen

"How did your date go?" Jennifer asked the following morning.

"The date," Tracy said, with a hint of a smile, "was a disaster."

"So how come you look so happy?"

"Jennifer, I was up most of the night moping about what an awful time I had. But around three o'clock, I wised up and realized I had nothing to feel sorry about. See, a month ago, I would have let a guy like Sting walk all over me. But last night I didn't. It doesn't make what happened any better, but for once I feel good about it."

"Good for you." Jennifer patted Tracy's shoulder. "Too bad about the date, though. I thought the third time was supposed to be the charm,"

"Sting wouldn't know charm if it fell on him. Unfortunately, things are still the same with David. I don't know what I'm going to do." She paused to mop her forehead. "Is it me, or is it like a furnace in here?"

"For once it's not you," Margaret said, overhearing Tracy's last statement on her way to the kitchen.

"Bad news, girls," Hilda announced, approaching from Mr. Parron's rear office. "The air conditioner broke down, and it may take hours to get someone to fix it. Let's hope the sea breeze can cool it down in here. Come help me open the windows."

The hot weather seemed to get on everyone's nerves that morning. Nearly all of Tracy's customers complained, and she patiently had to explain the situation.

"I want to see Captain Tony himself," one customer told her.

"I'm sorry, sir, you can't."

"Well, why not?"

"Captain Tony is dead, sir."

"Not surprised," the man grumbled. "This heat is enough to kill anyone."

At ten-thirty Hilda asked Tracy to refill the sugar jars. Tracy was glad to be busy, although work wasn't enough to free her mind from constant thoughts of David. She had tried to speak to him all morning, but every time she'd come near, he had turned to the other side of the grill.

An hour later, after completing her assignment, Tracy had enough time to freshen up in the ladies' room and pull her hair into a more comfortable ponytail. She splashed some cold water on her face, both to cool off and to rouse herself from the fatigue that was beginning to catch up with her from her lack of sleep.

By the time she reentered the dining room, the whole place was filled with senior citizens.

Tracy took the orders from the first table and retreated to the kitchen. If it was hot in the main room, it was sweltering in there. The two cooks and dishwasher had stripped down to their T-shirts. David's head was sopping wet, and he looked so uncomfortable Tracy felt sorry for him. But he was concentrating on his cooking, seemingly oblivious to his surroundings—and to her. Sadly, Tracy placed her orders on the clip and headed for her next table.

On Tracy's next trip to the kitchen, she dropped off some more slips, then carefully loaded the salad orders onto a tray. As she turned toward the door, she stepped right into a slick puddle.

She gasped as she lost her balance and fell to the floor. The platter came down on top of her, dishes shattering all around her.

Mr. Parron put in an appearance immediately. "Miss Fox!" he shouted angrily. "What's going on here?"

"I slipped, sir. I'm—"

"You're fired, young woman. I told you—"

"Walter, wait a minute." Tracy looked up at Hilda, who had joined him in the kitchen. "I think you owe Tracy another chance."

"What?" He looked at Hilda oddly, his cigar dangling from his mouth.

"You heard me," Hilda said. "Tracy's become one of our best waitresses. This was just an accident."

"That's right, Mr. Parron." Tracy was surprised to hear David's voice. "Look," he said, pointing, "she must have slipped in this puddle. It could have happened to anyone. If it's the broken dishes you're worried about, I'll pay for them. And for the food, too, if it matters."

"I'll chip in," Jennifer said, approaching the group.

Mr. Parron looked at them both. "That won't be necessary," he said.

"Walter?" Hilda pleaded.

Mr. Parron took a puff on his cigar and

glared at Tracy. "All right. Clean up this mess as fast as you can. Then get back to your tables. That goes for all of you." Turning on his heel, he left.

Still on the floor, Tracy looked up at Hilda. "Does that mean I still have my job?"

Hilda smiled and pointed a thumb in the air.

"Thanks, Hilda. Thanks, everybody," she said.

"Here, let me help you up," David said.

Tracy felt a spark when he took hold of her arm. "I seem to keep getting into these messes." Tracy wiped a few flecks of tuna off her uniform.

"And I seem to keep helping you pick up the pieces."

"And the shrimp," Tracy added.

"No, I'll leave that to you. I've got a few thousand meals to put together." Leaning closer to her, he added in a whisper, "We've got to talk. Let's meet in the lobby after work."

Tracy smiled. "I thought you'd never ask."

She quickly cleaned up the mess in the kitchen, Jennifer having volunteered to take care of her tables in the meantime. She couldn't stop thinking about David and their meeting. She didn't know what he was going to say, but the fact that he wanted to speak to her gave her renewed hope.

"Well, here I am," she said, meeting David at the scheduled hour.

"I don't know about you, but I've got to get out of this place."

"Let's go down to the jetty," Tracy suggested.

"That's exactly what I was thinking."

But David couldn't wait to say what was on his mind. As they strolled down the boardwalk, he said, "I realized something this afternoon."

"What?"

"I'm crazy about you, Tracy Fox. I haven't stopped thinking about you for days, and when I saw you flat on your back and about to be fired, I realized I couldn't survive the rest of the summer without seeing you again."

"Oh, David, you don't know how happy I am to hear that," Tracy said, beaming.

They reached the entrance to the beach, took off their shoes, and walked down three steps into the hot sand. "Yipes!" Tracy screamed. "Last one to the jetty is a rotten egg!" Without waiting for a response, she sped across the beach, stopping only when she could bury her toes in the wet sand near the ocean.

"Whew," David breathed, catching up with her. "This is a day for the record books. I may take a dip with all my clothes on."

"Wait a second," Tracy said. "You started something back there. I'd like to hear the end of it."

David ambled over to the nearest rock and leaned on it. "What can I say? I like you. I can see why other guys like you, too." He shrugged.

"But, David, it's just you I want. When I told you about those other dates, I failed to mention one other little piece of information."

"Oh?"

"I didn't want to tell you this because I knew you weren't going to like it. See, you may have noticed I haven't invited you to my house yet. It's because of my mother. She's gotten it into her head that a townie's not good enough for me."

"That's ridiculous."

"Of course it is, and I've tried to tell her that if she met you she'd change her mind in a second. But she's like a mule on this."

"Is that why you went on the date?"

"Yes. My mother decided this was going to be the summer Tracy Fox learned how to be sophisticated. She figured any boy who was the son of someone she admired would be full of sophistication and somehow it would rub off on me." She kicked her foot in the sand. "A lot she knows. Three boys—and each one a bigger jerk than the last. I tried to get out of it, out of every date, I really did, but she begged me to keep trying. I—I just couldn't say no."

"And I wasn't much help, was I?"

"No, but I understand how you felt. I'd probably have reacted the same way."

David sighed. He looked at Tracy for a long, long time. Finally he said, "So there's no way your mother will accept me—just because I'm a local."

"Crazy, but true."

He motioned her close and held her for a long time. "What are we going to do?"

"I don't know, David. She's not trying to be mean—I mean, she never said I *couldn't* date you. But it's like she prefers to pretend you don't exist. The funny thing is, you've got more going for you in your little finger than any of those boys can ever hope for."

"I wish there was a way we could make her see that," he said.

Tracy hugged him tighter. "Don't worry, David. I'll think of something."

Chapter Seventeen

Tracy greeted Dina at the restaurant about a week later. "I'm really glad you could come down here on such short notice," she said, leading her to a vacant table near the bar.

"I told my boss I was taking an early lunch," Dina said. "You sounded desperate on the phone. What's wrong?"

"I need your help. I've got an idea how I can get Mom to accept David."

"Hmm, this sounds interesting," Dina said.

"I've got to talk fast. I'm on my break, and I don't have much time." She took a deep breath. "What if we could fix it so Mom thought David was a charming, cultured boy of the world?"

"What do you mean?"

"Well, David is cultured in a way—at least

enough for me. And he's good-looking, intelligent, and a gourmet cook. But what he isn't, is from out of town—and that's where I could use your help."

"I see," Dina said, brightening. "You want me to pretend he's a friend of mine from somewhere exotic, right?"

"Something like that," Tracy said excitedly. "See, if you tell Mom you've got this terrific guy for me, she's bound to be interested."

"Even though she knows the way you feel about these fix-ups?" Dina asked.

"I've got that covered, too. You can tell her all about David's cooking abilities and suggest that instead of a date, he come over to our house and fix a dinner for us. No obligations on anyone's part. Tell her he said that if I don't like him or he doesn't like me, he'll pack up his things and call it a night as soon as dinner's over. She'll think that's really reasonable and try to get me to go along. I'll put up a fuss, of course, but agree to it in the end. What do you say?"

"You do think of everything, don't you?" Dina said, smiling. "But I'm not so sure, Tracy."

"Oh, you've got to help!" Tracy cried, rising. "Stay right here. I'm going to get David.

138

Once you meet him, you'll see why I'm resorting to a desperate act like this."

Tracy rushed to the kitchen and coaxed David away from the fried fish batter he was mixing. "It's just for a minute," she told him. "I've almost got Dina sold on the idea, but she wants to meet you first."

"OK, Tracy."

Grabbing his hand, she led him out the kitchen door. They had just turned the bend toward the lounge area when Tracy made a quick about-face and pushed him back toward the kitchen.

"Stay here and don't go out there," she warned when they were back inside.

"I thought you were taking me to Dina. What's going on?"

"That's what I'd like to know," she said. "I just saw my mother out there!"

Tracy reentered the dining room and saw her mother standing next to Dina near a table in the cocktail lounge. Her mother was carrying a stack of folders in one arm. Behind her, Gopher was stringing a black wire around the perimeter of the room.

"Hi, Mom," Tracy said, giving her a quick hug. "What are you doing here?"

"We're running the show out of here today," she said. "Didn't I tell you?"

"No."

Her mother dropped the files on the table. "I don't know where my head is sometimes," she said. "We've had this planned for days. Besides, I thought it was about time I got to see you at work."

"You're welcome to watch," Tracy said, "but I imagine it's pretty boring."

"Nancy," Gopher said, placing a microphone on the table, "I need some tests now. Do you mind?"

She shrugged. "I've got to get back to work, Tracy."

"Yeah, me, too. I'll see you later."

Before she returned to her tables, Tracy managed a final word with Dina. "You didn't tell her anything, did you?" she asked.

"Oh, no," Dina said. "She was surprised to see me here, but I told her a story about having to stop at Lloyd's and deciding to drop in on you on the spur of the moment."

"Whew," Tracy breathed. "That was close."

"By the way, I've been thinking about your plan. Let's try it. I think it would be fun."

Tracy squeezed her hands. "Thank you! You're a lifesaver."

Grinning broadly, Tracy met David early the next morning. "It worked!" she announced gleefully. "You and I have a date for Saturday night."

"You mean your mom didn't catch on?" David asked.

"Not in the slightest. I put up a stink at first, but her selling job was too hard to resist. She really thinks you're some marvelous find of Dina's. Not to mention a 'gourmet.'"

"I've got to hand it to you. When you came up with this idea, I thought you were a little crazy. But I have a feeling it might work out."

"All I did was start thinking like my mother. The rest was easy."

"I've already got the menu planned. She'd better love to eat."

Chapter Eighteen

Tracy rushed home from work on Saturday, anxious to look her best for the "date." She stood looking in her closet for five minutes before she chose her blue plaid prairie skirt and white ruffled blouse. She tied a blue bow in her hair, spent nearly an hour putting on her eye makeup, and for a final touch, slipped on a cameo necklace Jennifer had given her as a good-luck charm.

"Tracy, you look marvelous," her mother said when she peeked into the bathroom. "I was wondering what you were doing in here."

"I figured if this boy is going to go to all the trouble of cooking us a dinner, the least I could do was dress properly for it."

"He ought to be here any minute."

"I'll be ready," Tracy said. Looking at her

mother, she added, "You look pretty nice yourself."

Seconds later, the doorbell rang. "Dina, how are you?" Nancy Fox said, hugging her friend. Turning to the tall boy who stood next to her carrying a big box, she added, "Welcome—oh, I don't believe Dina told me your name."

"Chip," he answered. "Pleased to meet you, Mrs. Fox. Sorry I can't shake your hand. I've got four stuffed cornish hens in here."

"Please come inside. That must be heavy."

"Oh, no. Down at the res—um, at home I do a lot of cooking and carrying things around." David's face reddened a little. "Where's the kitchen?"

"Come with me." Nancy led him to the back of the house.

Dina, meanwhile, greeted Tracy, complimenting her on her outfit and adding, "Did you see the way she lit up when he smiled at her?"

"I told you David was a charmer," Tracy whispered. "I just hope that wasn't one of my mother's professionally gracious looks."

"Seemed real to me," Dina said. "This just might work, Tracy."

"It better. It's going to be hard to pretend I don't know him, though."

143

"I'll run interference if you need it," Dina offered.

Tracy took her arm. "C'mon, let's see what they're up to in there."

Swinging open the door, Tracy heard her mother telling David, ". . . and I always found the most marvelous fruits and vegetables on Ninth Avenue."

David was filling a pot with water. "I've discovered the best vegetables are the ones you grow yourself."

"So you're a gardener, too?" Tracy's mother sounded impressed.

"Actually, the garden is my mother's project, but I help out every now and then." Turning to the stove, he made eye contact with Tracy. "Is this your daughter?"

Tracy's mother smiled proudly. "Chip, I'd like you to meet Tracy."

"How do you do?" she said, suppressing a giggle.

"I hope you like cornish game hens. I've just got to prepare the broccoli and sauce, and we'll be all ready to go."

"That sounds delicious. Need any help, *Chip*?" Tracy asked.

"Not really, but you're welcome to watch. Dina tells me you work in a restaurant."

"For the summer," she said. She tried hard

144

to keep a straight face. "I serve the food, though I don't cook it."

David took a carton of cream from the bag he'd brought along. "Where could I find a saucepan?"

"Right here." Tracy's mother reached inside one of the lower cabinets and pulled out a one-quart pot.

"Thanks. I really like your kitchen."

"Yes, there's lots of room to stretch out," Tracy's mother said.

David stirred a few spices into the simmering sauce.

"Mmm, that smells delicious," Tracy's mother said. "Cooking must be a serious hobby of yours."

"Actually, I plan to make it my life's work. Study with some fine chefs and then open a restaurant of my own."

"I like a boy with ambition."

"That sounds fascinating," Tracy spoke up, just to let everyone know she was still alive.

"Tracy, do you have salad bowls? We'll need them tonight," David said.

"Sure, Dav—Chip," she corrected herself.

Within minutes the meal was ready. Over dinner, Tracy's mother continued to grill David about his background. "Dina never did tell me where you live," she remarked.

"In New Jersey," he answered, adding quickly, "Please tell me about your radio show. It sounds really interesting."

So Nancy launched into a series of stories about the guests she had interviewed recently.

Finally she stopped and beckoned to Tracy. "Come help me clear these dishes."

In the kitchen she whispered excitedly, "Well, what do you think?"

"He's not bad."

"Is that all you can say?" She looked at her daughter incredulously.

"He's not a bad cook," Tracy went on. "And he did seem interested in me. He's not bad-looking, either—"

"Tracy, I may only be your mother, but my eyes tell me this one is a terrific catch. What could you possibly find wrong with him?"

"Nothing . . . so far. I just don't like rushing into things. But," she added, "I think I'll give him a try, if you like."

Over chocolate mousse and coffee, Tracy said to David, "There's a terrific video parlor on the boardwalk. It's got everything. Would you like to check it out?"

"Sounds like fun," he said.

Nancy looked at them and sighed contentedly. "Don't worry about the dishes. Dina and I will clean up. Have fun, you two."

Tracy and David waited until they got to the end of the block before bursting into laughter. "For a while there, I didn't think I was going to make it," Tracy said between gasps.

"It was awful hard pretending not to know you. That's why I concentrated so much of my attention on your mother."

"Well, it worked. By the way, where'd you come up with Chip, anyway?"

"I was afraid she might put two and two together if I introduced myself as David. Chip was a nickname I had when I was a kid."

"Chip, David, whatever. Mom told me I was crazy if I decided not to take advantage of the opportunity of dating you."

"That is one point I agree with your mother on." David smiled. "She is rather fascinating—once you get past her ideas about boys."

"Like I told you, it's just a phase she's going through. Until this summer she didn't care who I went out with. But I'm glad she finally got the opportunity to meet you."

The video parlor was so crowded that Tracy and David decided not to go inside. "What do you say we just walk along the boardwalk for a little while?" he suggested.

Tracy pulled her sweater a little tighter.

"Fine with me, but it feels like it's going to rain."

"Let it," David said. "Nothing could dampen my spirits now."

Silently they passed by the closed bathhouse and the souvenir shops. David put his arm around Tracy's waist to shield her from the gently rising wind. Her pace began to slow, however, as she guided him to the railing that separated the boardwalk from the beach. With the wind now blowing directly into her face, she stared out into the choppy water.

"A penny for your thoughts?" David asked.

"Huh-uh, nothing for less than a nickel," she said. Then, sighing, she added, "I was just thinking about tonight. I'm starting to feel a little funny about tricking my mother."

"It wasn't really a trick."

"What do *you* call pretending to be someone you weren't?"

"But I wasn't pretending to be someone else. I was myself."

"Chip? From someplace in New Jersey? You can't deny there was a bit of subterfuge involved."

"But we had no other choice."

"I know. Still, I feel funny about it all. I've never lied to her like this before." She felt a drop hit her forehead.

148

"You didn't have anything to do with it. Dina brought me there. I did my little performance."

"It was my idea, David." She held out her hand to feel the rain. "I think we ought to go back and tell her the truth."

"Why?"

"Because I'll feel better. The one thing I never did in all this time was to bring you home and make her see you as you are. Maybe if I had, we never would have had to go through all this." She turned back toward her house.

"But what if she gets mad and kicks me out?"

"That's a chance we've got to take. All I know is if we don't do this, I'll have a hard time looking her in the face again."

The two of them headed for Tracy's house just as the skies opened up.

Chapter Nineteen

Tracy and David were soaked from head to foot by the time they reached her front door.

"My goodness, look what the cat dragged in," her mother exclaimed.

Dina called from the living room, "I'll put up the hot water and make you some tea."

"Thanks," Tracy called. A small pool was forming underneath her.

"Here, wipe off, you two," her mother said, handing them both towels. "You're home pretty early."

"The Video Shack was a zoo, so we didn't stay long. Then we got caught in the rain."

"Chip, you're drenched. I'd offer you a change of clothes, but . . ."

David smiled. "Oh, I'll be all right."

"Sit down, Mom," Tracy said abruptly. "I've

got something to tell you." She draped a fresh towel over one of the wing chairs before taking a seat.

"Is something wrong, Tracy?"

"Well, I did something tonight I'm ashamed of now," she began.

"What is it, dear?" her mother asked, concerned.

"Before I tell you, I want to let you know why I felt I had to do it. You see, all summer long you've been trying to push boys on me, even after I told you I wasn't interested in them."

"Tracy, are you sure you want to talk about this now?" her mother asked, glancing at David sitting in the other wing chair.

"Yes. I have to. Mom, you had this idea in your head that I needed to be exposed to culture and new ideas and new people. I'm sorry I'm not the sophisticated person you want me to be. But I have enough trouble just being Tracy Fox, without having to add on another layer, especially one I don't feel."

"I've really made a mess of things, haven't I?" her mother said.

"Look, Mom, as much as I want to, I'll never be as perfect as you."

"Tracy, I never felt there was anything wrong with you," her mother asserted. "And me, perfect? Believe me, Tracy, I have many faults. Maybe one of them is thinking I'm the only one who knows what kind of boy is right for you."

"You meant well—and I love you for that," Tracy said. "But I learned something from those dates, something you never counted on. People aren't desirable just because they come from a rich family or wear the right clothes or speak with a foreign accent. All I want is someone who is caring, someone who has a good sense of who he is and what he wants out of life. And if that's not good enough for you, then I'm sorry, because I think it's good enough for me."

She took a deep breath. "Anyway, I met someone this summer I like a lot—even though he doesn't have much money or a car or an exotic name. Mom, this isn't Chip. This is David Saylor, the boy I've been telling you about." Although Tracy felt as if she had just lifted a load off her chest, she dreaded her mother's response.

"I know, dear."

Tracy looked up, stunned. "You *what*?"

Nancy smiled slowly. "I should have known you could handle your own love life. Still, it bothered me to see you growing up so fast—and me having so little to do with it. With all the work I've put in at the radio station, I felt I'd neglected to teach you some of the things I always wanted you to know, the things that living in a small town like this can't teach you. I know now I was wrong. Do you think you could forgive your old mother for her dumb mistakes?"

"Oh, Mom." Tracy rose to hug her mother. "There's nothing to forgive. But how did you know this was David?"

"You shouldn't leave snapshots of your boyfriends around so your snoopy mother can find them." She took a picture of David out of her pocket.

Tracy gulped. "So we didn't fool you after all."

"No, but I enjoyed every minute of it."

"And you're not mad at me?" Tracy asked.

"As a mother, I should be, but after what I've done, I suppose I deserve it."

"Besides, she'd have to punish me, too," Dina said, carrying in a tray of steaming tea.

"And me," David added.

"But the other part of it is," Nancy Fox added, smiling, "it reminds me of something similar I pulled on Grandma once."

"See, Tracy?" David spoke up. "You're more like your mother than you thought."

Turning to David, Tracy's mother added, "I

really did love your dinner. You'll have to come back soon and let me cook for *you*. I've got a few good recipes of my own."

"I'd like that a lot, Mrs. Fox."

"I think the best thing I could do now is have a cup of tea in the kitchen with Dina and let you two continue your date." She rose.

Tracy led David out to the loveseat on the porch. They sat down together, and Tracy smiled. "I think she likes you," she whispered.

"What's more important is that she likes you—just the way you are," David said. "And by the way, I think she has excellent taste." David tilted Tracy's chin upward and gave her a long, lingering kiss.

"Ooh, I liked that," Tracy said when they parted.

Snuggled deep in David's embrace, Tracy sighed peacefully, thinking that the best days of summer were yet to come.